BACK
STORY

BACK STORY

Robert B. Parker

Thorndike Press   **Chivers Press**
Waterville, Maine USA   **Bath, England**

This Large Print edition is published by Thorndike Press®, USA and by Chivers Press, England.

Published in 2003 in the U.S. by arrangement with G. P. Putnam's Sons, a member of Penguin Group (USA) Inc.

Published in 2003 in the U.K. by arrangement with John Murray (Publishers) Ltd.

U.S. Hardcover 0-7862-5451-3 (Basic Series)
U.K. Hardcover 0-7540-1989-6 (Windsor Large Print)
U.K. Softcover 0-7540-9337-9 (Paragon Large Print)

Copyright © 2003 by Robert B. Parker
A Spenser Novel

All rights reserved.

The text of this Large Print edition is unabridged. Other aspects of the book may vary from the original edition.

Set in 16 pt. Plantin by Elena Picard.

Printed in the United States on permanent paper.

British Library Cataloguing-in-Publication Data available

Library of Congress Cataloging-in-Publication Data

Parker, Robert B., 1932–
    Back story / Robert B. Parker.
        p. cm.
    ISBN 0-7862-5451-3 (lg. print : hc : alk. paper)
    1. Spenser (Fictitious character) — Fiction. 2. Private investigators — Massachusetts — Boston — Fiction.
3. Boston (Mass.) — Fiction. 4. Large type books.
I. Title.
PS3566.A686B33 2003
813'.54—dc21   2003047869

Joan: Every Year Variety More Infinite

1

♦ ♦ ♦ ♦ ♦

It was a late May morning in Boston. I had coffee. I was sitting in my swivel chair, with my feet up, looking out my window at the Back Bay. The lights were on in my office. Outside, the temperature was 53. The sky was low and gray. There was no rain yet, but the air was swollen with it, and I knew it would come. Across Boylston, on the other side of Berkeley Street, I saw Paul Giacomin walking with a dark-haired woman. They stopped at the light and, when it changed, came on across toward my office. They both moved well, like people who'd been trained. I'd have to see her close-up to confirm, but from here I thought the woman looked good. I was pleased to see that Paul was carrying a paper bag. I swiveled my chair back around and, by the time they got up to my office, I was standing in the doorway. Paul smiled and handed me the bag.

"Krispy Kremes?" I said.

"Like always," he said.

I put the bag on my desk and turned

back and hugged Paul.

"This is Daryl Silver," Paul said.

"My real name is Gordon," she said. "Silver is my professional name."

We shook hands. Daryl was, in fact, a knockout. Eagle-eye Spenser. I opened the paper bag and took out a cardboard box of donuts.

"They haven't got these yet in Boston," Paul told Daryl. "So whenever I come home, I bring some."

"Will you join me?" I said to Daryl.

"Thanks," she said. "I'd love to."

"That's a major compliment," Paul said to her. "Usually he goes off in a corner and eats them all."

I poured us some coffee. Paul was looking at the picture on top of the file cabinet of Susan, Pearl, and me.

"I'm sorry about Pearl," Paul said.

"Thank you."

"You okay?"

I shrugged and nodded.

"Susan?"

I shrugged and held out the box of donuts.

"Krispy Kreme?" I said.

The rain arrived and released some of the tension in the atmosphere. It rained first in small, incoherent splatters on the window, then more steadily, then hard. It was very dark out, and the lights in my office seemed warm.

"How did it go in Chicago?" I said.

"The play got good notices," Paul said.

"You read them?"

"No. But people tell me."

"You like directing?"

"I think so. But it's my own play. I don't know if I'd want to direct something written by somebody else."

"How's rehearsal going here?"

"We've done the play too often," Paul said. "We're having trouble with our energy."

"And you're in this?" I said to Daryl.

"Yes."

"She's gotten really great reviews," Paul said. "In Chicago, and before that in Louisville."

"I have good lines to speak," she said.

"Well, yeah," Paul said. "There's that."

With the rain falling, the air had loosened. Below my window, most of the cars had their lights on, and the wet pavement shimmered pleasantly. The lights at Boylston Street, diffused by the rain, looked like bright flowers.

"Daryl would like to talk to you about something," Paul said.

"Sure," I said.

Paul looked at her and nodded. She took in a deep breath.

"Twenty-eight years ago my mother was murdered," she said.

After twenty-eight years, "I'm sorry" seemed aimless.

"1974," I said.

"Yes. In September. She was shot down in a bank in Boston, by people robbing it."

I nodded.

"For no good reason."

I nodded again. There was rarely a good reason.

"I want them found."

"I don't blame you," I said. "But why now, after twenty-eight years?"

"I didn't know how to do it or who to ask. Then I met Paul and he told me about you. He said you saved his life."

"He might exaggerate a little," I said.

"He said if they could be found, you could find them."

"He might exaggerate a little."

"We lived in La Jolla," Daryl said. "We were visiting my mother's sister in Boston. My mother just went into the bank to cash some traveler's checks. And they shot her."

"Were you with her?" I said.

"No. The police told me. I was with my aunt."

"How old were you when your mother died?"

"Six."

"And you still can't let it go," I said.

"I'll never let it go."

I drank some coffee. There were two Krispy Kremes left in the box. I had already eaten one more than either of my guests.

"Either of you want another donut?" I said.

They didn't. I felt the warm pleasure of relief spread through me. I didn't take a donut. I just sipped a little coffee. I didn't want to seem too eager.

"I remember it," I said. "Old Shawmut Bank branch in Audubon Circle. It's a restaurant now."

"Yes."

"Some sort of revolutionary group."

"The Dread Scott Brigade."

"Ah, yes," I said.

"You know of them?"

"Those were heady times," I said, "for groups with funny names."

I reached over casually, as if I weren't even thinking about it, and took one of the donuts.

11

"I can't pay you very much," she said.

"She can't pay you anything," Paul said.

"Solve a thirty-year-old murder for no money," I said. "How enticing."

Daryl looked down at her hands, folded in her lap.

"I know," she said.

"Awhile ago, I did a thing for Rita Fiore," I said to Paul, "and last week her firm finally got around to paying me."

"A lot?"

"Yes," I said. "A lot."

Paul grinned. "Timing is everything," he said.

"Does that mean you'll help me?" Daryl said.

"It does," I said.

2

I met Martin Quirk for a drink in a bar in South Boston called Arno's, where a lot of cops had started to hang out since Police Headquarters had been conveniently relocated to South Cove. I got there first and was drinking a draft Budweiser when Quirk arrived. He was a big guy, about my size, and you could tell he was strong. But mostly what you noticed was how implacable he seemed. Several cops greeted him carefully. When he sat beside me, the bartender came quickly down the bar.

"What'll it be, Captain?"

"Ketel One on the rocks, with a twist," Quirk said.

"You got it, Captain."

"Sorry about your dog," Quirk said to me.

"Thank you."

"You and Susan going to get another one?"

"Yes."

"You want to stop talking about this?"

"I do."

"Okay, whaddya need?"

13

Quirk's drink came promptly. He took a sip, swallowed, and smiled to himself.

"I found myself missing you, Captain."

"Sure," Quirk said. "Happens all the time."

He took another sip of his vodka. Quirk had hands like a stone mason, but all his movements were quite delicate.

"In 1974," I said. "A woman named Emily Gordon was shot by a group called the Dread Scott Brigade who were holding up a bank in Audubon Circle."

"Nobody ever saw who shot her. Everyone was lying facedown on the floor."

"You remember every case?" I said.

"I remember that. It was before I started working Homicide full-time. I was working detectives out of old Station Sixteen, you remember, before we reorganized?"

I nodded.

"I was one of the guys who responded when the call came in."

"Were you on it all the way?"

"No. Homicide Division took it over. But I always kind of followed the thing."

The television was on behind the bar, and the early newscasters were in a frenzy over the possibility of showers on the weekend.

"Homicide get anywhere?" I said.

14

"Couldn't find them," Quirk said. "Had pictures from the bank security cameras. Had eyewitnesses. Had a letter from the Dread Scott Brigade saying they did it. Dread, by the way is spelled e-a-d."

"Why, those clever punsters," I said. "Did it mention Emily Gordon?"

"I think it said something about how no member of the oppressor class is safe."

"How 1974 is that?" I said.

"They spelled oppression wrong," Quirk said.

"So Homicide think they've got a no-brainer," I said.

"Bunch of fucking amateurs," Quirk said. "Up against a crew of street-smart big-city homicide dicks." He drank another sip of his vodka.

"And?" I said.

"Amateurs one," Quirk said. "Dicks nothing."

"So far," I said.

"So far," Quirk said. "Being amateurs actually helped them."

"No MO," I said. "No arrest record. No mug shots to compare with the bank photos."

"Nobody recognized them," Quirk said. "The FBI never heard of them."

"They claim credit for any other jobs?" I said.

"Not that I know."

"Money ever show up?"

"Nope. But you know how that works. How many people get cash and check the serial numbers."

"Banks do," I said.

"Banks say they do," Quirk said.

My beer was gone. I gestured to the bartender for another one. The bartender picked up my glass and looked at Quirk. Quirk shook his head and the bartender went to draw me another Bud. I still preferred Blue Moon Belgian White Ale. But that was not one of the options at Arno's. In fact, Budweiser *was* the option.

"Murder weapon?" I said.

"Yep, and the car they used."

"Prints on the gun?"

"Gun was clean," Quirk said.

"Car?" I said.

"Most of the prints in the car belonged to the guy they stole it from."

"Trace the gun?"

"Yep. M1 carbine. Fully automatic. Stolen from a National Guard Armory in Akron, Ohio, in 1963."

"So who was in the bank?" I said.

"A black guy. A white woman. There was probably someone driving the car, but no one saw who it was."

"And that's it?" I said. "That's all there is?"

"That's absolutely fucking it," Quirk said.

"Anyone remember who had the carbine?"

"Far as I can tell, all of them had long guns. Nobody in there knew one from another," Quirk said. "Homicide never got a sniff."

"And they were on it when it was hot."

"Uh-huh."

"I'm starting out after it's been cold for twenty-eight years."

"You working for someone?"

"Emily Gordon's daughter is a friend of Paul Giacomin's," I said.

"Oh," Quirk said.

"Oh," I said.

"How is the kid?"

"Paul? He's not a kid anymore."

"I know how that works," Quirk said. "Two of my kids are older than I am."

"Anything else you can tell me, gimme someplace to start?"

"I told you what I remember," Quirk said. "You want to come in, you can look at the case files."

"I will," I said.

"She paying you top dollar for this?" Quirk said.

"She and Paul gave me six donuts this morning."

Quirk nodded thoughtfully.

"Yeah," he said. "That would buy you."

3

♦ ♦ ♦ ♦ ♦

I sat at an empty desk in the Homicide Division outside Quirk's office. There were a lot of other desks in neat rows under bright lights. The floor was clean. The file cabinets were new. All the desks had computers on them. The old Berkeley Street headquarters was cramped and unattractive and looked like what it was. This place looked like a room for stockbrokers with bright suspenders and cuff links. Cops weren't supposed to be working under these conditions. I felt like I was in L.A. The file on Emily Gordon's murder was in a big brown cardboard envelope closed with a thick rubber band. It had never been computerized. I was grateful at least for that.

A detective named DeLong walked past and stopped and came back. He had on a green Lacoste polo shirt hanging over blue jeans. I could see the outline of his gun, in front, under the shirttail.

"Spenser," he said. "You re-upping?"

"Just stopped by to give you guys a hand," I said.

"Don't steal anything," DeLong said.

I looked around the Homicide Division. "Place is an embarrassment, DeLong."

"Yeah. I know. I'm turning into a sissy."

"You remember a bank robbery in Audubon Circle, in 1974? Woman got killed."

"1974? For crissake, Spenser, I was fifteen in 1974."

"Yeah," I said. "Me too."

DeLong looked like he was going to say something, then shook his head and walked off. I went back to my case file. Aside from the autopsy report and the crime scene write-up, the case file was mostly reports written by Mario Bennati, detective first grade. I didn't know him. Quirk said he had been the lead detective on the case and that he'd retired in 1982. I plowed along. Cops aren't usually graceful writers, and the jargon of investigative procedure didn't help. For a case that had no clues, no identifiable suspects, and no resolution, there was a lot of stuff, none of it helpful. Bennati had tried. His case log showed he had talked to all the customers in the bank, everyone he could find who'd been in the vicinity of the bank, and all bank employees. He'd talked to Emily Gordon's sister, Sybil Gold, to six-year-old Daryl Gordon, and to Emily Gordon's husband, Barry, from whom she had apparently been estranged at the time of the shooting. There had been talk with the FBI. The FBI would send over an intelligence report on the Dread Scott Brigade. There had been talk with the cops in San Diego. Talk with the DEA. Talk with the Army about the stolen carbine. Talk with the bank examiners. All the statements were included. I ploughed on. It was late afternoon. I needed a nap.

I drank a lot of bad coffee. The night watch came on. I was hungry. When I finally finished, it was dark outside. I closed the envelope and put it on the empty desk and leaned my head back against the chair and closed my eyes and took in some long, quiet breaths.

Where was the FBI intelligence report?

4

Quirk was still in his office, his jacket hung on a hanger on the back of his door. His feet were on the desk, his tie was loosened, his shirt cuffs rolled. He was looking at a large bulletin board across the small room, where a number of crime scene photographs were posted.

"You still here?" he said.

"You ever read this case file?" I said.

"Yes."

He kept staring at the photographs.

"Anything bother you in there?"

"Like what?"

"Like the FBI intelligence report."

"Ah," Quirk said, still scanning the pictures. "You spotted that, too."

"Any thoughts?" I said.

"Nope."

"You ever chase it down?"

"I never saw the case file until I got to be Homicide Commander. By then the case was cold. Command staff don't much like it when the Homicide Commander, the new Homicide Commander, starts up with the Feds over a cold, cold case we never solved."

"Politics affects police work?" I said.

"Shocking, isn't it. How was it when you were a cop?"

"Politics affected police work," I said.

"How disappointing," Quirk said.

"Lead investigator was a guy named Bennati," I said. "He still around?"

"Retired," Quirk said. "Lives up on the North Shore now."

I looked at Quirk. He was scanning the crime scene photos again.

"That's why you offered me the case files," I said.

"Spirit of cooperation," Quirk said.

"That FBI reference bothered you, too, but it didn't seem like a good idea to pursue it. But you don't forget anything. So when I finally came along . . ."

Quirk continued to study the photos.

"I'm supposed to be an executive now," Quirk said. "Manage the division. Let the detectives do most of the hands-on stuff. But I like to stay late, couple nights a week, and look at the crime scene coverage while it's quiet, and see what I can see."

I nodded.

"Woman and two children killed in this one," Quirk said, nodding at the pictures.

"Woman was raped first."

"I'll call you tomorrow," I said. "Get Bennati's address."

"Call Belson," Quirk said. "He'll get it for you."

5

♦ ♦ ♦ ♦ ♦

Mario Bennati lived in Gloucester in a small, gray-shingled house with a deck where you could sit and drink beer and look at the Annisquam River. He and I were sitting there, doing that, in the late afternoon. With us was a large friendly German shepherd named Grover.

"Wife died four years ago," Bennati said. "Daughter comes up from Stoughton usually once or twice a week, vacuums, dusts. . . ." He shrugged. "Mostly it's me and Grover. I can cook okay and do my laundry."

We were drinking Miller High Life from the clear glass bottles.

"I don't smoke no more," he said, looking at the boats moving toward the harbor across the wide water below us. "Ain't got laid since she died." He drank some of the Miller High Life with an economy of motion that suggested long practice. "We done fine, 'fore she got sick." Grover put his head on Bennati's thigh and looked at him. "Watch this," Bennati said.

He tilted the bottle of beer carefully and Grover drank a little. "Right from the bottle," Bennati said. "Huh?"

"Cool," I said.

"Don't let him drink much," Bennati said. "Gets drunk real easy."

I patted Grover on the backside. His tail wagged, but he kept his head on Bennati's lap. "I'm looking into an old murder," I said. "One of yours. September 1974. Woman was killed in a bank holdup in Audubon Circle."

Bennati drank the rest of his beer and reached down and got another one out of the cooler under the table. He twisted off the cap and drank probably four ounces of the beer in one long pull. He looked at the bottle for a moment and nodded.

"Yeah, sure, bunch of fucking hippies," he said. "Stealing money to save America. Killed her for no good reason."

"I read the case file yesterday," I said.

"So you know we didn't clear it." He drank some more beer. "They're always a bitch, the fucking cases where shit happens for no good reason."

I nodded. "Anything you remember, might help me?" I said.

"You read the case file, you know what I know," he said.

"I used to be a cop," I said. "Everything didn't always get included in the case file."

"Did in mine," Bennati said.

"What happened to the FBI intelligence report?" I said.

"Huh?"

"In your notes you say the FBI was sending over an intelligence report. It's not in the file and you never mentioned it again."

"FBI?"

"Uh-huh."

"For crissake, we're talking like thirty fucking years ago."

"Twenty-eight," I said. "You remember anything about the FBI intelligence report?"

"Too long," he said. "I'm seventy-six years old and live alone except for the dog, and drink too much beer. I can barely remember where my dick is."

"So you don't remember the FBI report?"

"No," he said and looked at me steadily. "I don't remember."

I took a card out of my shirt pocket and gave it to him.

"Anything occurs to you," I said, "give me a buzz."

"Sure thing."

As I walked toward my car, he took another High Life out of the cooler and twisted off the cap.

6
♦ ♦ ♦ ♦ ♦

The Boston FBI office was in 1 Center Plaza. The agent in charge was a thin guy with receding hair and round eyeglasses with black rims named Nathan Epstein. It was like finding an Arab running a shul. We shook hands when I came in, and he gestured me to a chair.

"You're the SAC," I said.

"I am."

"At least tell me you went to BC," I said.

"Nope." He had a strong New York accent.

"Fordham?"

"NYU," Epstein said.

"This is very disconcerting," I said.

"I know," he said. "People usually assume I'm from Accountemps."

He was wearing a dark blue suit, a white shirt, and a powder-blue silk tie.

"I am looking into a murder during a bank holdup in 1974," I said.

"Tell me about it," Epstein said.

I told him about it.

"Why did she come to you," Epstein said

when I finished.

"Mutual friend."

"And why did you take it on?"

"Favor to the friend," I said.

"Favor to a friend?" Epstein said. "The case is twenty-eight years cold. You have some reason to think you can solve it?"

"Self-regard," I said.

Epstein smiled. "So they tell me," he said.

"You checked me out?"

"I called the Commissioner's Office, they bucked me over to the Homicide Commander."

"Martin Quirk," I said.

Epstein nodded.

"You check out everyone you have an appointment with?" I said.

"I remembered the name," Epstein said. There was something very penetrating about him.

"You recall the case?"

Epstein smiled and shook his head. "Wasn't with the Bureau then," he said.

"Would it be possible for me to get a copy of the case file?"

He sat and thought about it. He was a guy that was probably never entirely still. As he thought, he turned a ballpoint pen slowly in his hands, periodically tapping a little paradiddle with it on the thumbnail of his left hand. Then he leaned forward and pushed a big khaki envelope toward me, the kind that you close by wrapping a little string around a little button.

"Here's the file," he said.

"Quirk?" I said.

"He mentioned you might be looking into the Gordon killing."

"Have you read it?"

"The file?" Epstein said. "Yes. I read it this morning. I assume you've read the BPD case file."

"I have."

"You'll find this pretty much a recycle of that."

"Someplace I can sit and read this?"

"Outside office," Epstein said. "One of my administrative assistants is on vacation. My chief administrator will show you her desk."

"Was there a time when we would have called your chief administrator a secretary?"

Epstein smiled his thin smile and said, "Long ago."

I took the folder and stood.

"I think I know what you're looking for," Epstein said.

I raised my eyebrows and didn't say anything.

"I don't know where the Bureau intelligence report is either," he said.

"The one that was supposed to be delivered to Bennati?"

"Yes."

I sat back down, holding the file envelope. "You noticed," I said.

"I did."

I sat back in my chair. "You guys gathered intelligence on dissident groups," I said.

"Some," Epstein said.

"Some? For chrissakes, the Bureau probably had a file on the Beach Boys."

Epstein smiled again . . . I think.

"Things have changed in the Bureau since those days."

"Sure," I said. "So do you have a file on the Dread Scott Brigade?"

"None that I know of."

"Could there be one you might not know of?"

"Of course."

"If there was one, how would I access it?"

"You'd get me to request it through channels," Epstein said.

"Will you?"

"I did."

"And?"

Epstein drummed on his thumbnail with his pen. His face was completely without expression.

"There appears to be no such file," he said.

"So how come Bennati thought one was on its way?"

"That is bothersome," Epstein said. "Isn't it."

7

♦ ♦ ♦ ♦ ♦

I drove up to Toronto on a Monday morning, with the sun shining the way it was supposed to in May, and got an all-chocolate, fifteen-month-old female German short-haired pointer, whose kennel name was Robin Hood's Purple Sandpiper. She was crated when I got her, which was a sound idea given that it was a ten-hour drive home. You wouldn't want her jumping around in a strange car and causing an accident. As I pulled onto 404 north of Toronto, she whimpered. At the first rest area we came to on 401, I discarded the crate next to the Dumpster behind the food court, and Robin Hood's Purple Sandpiper spent the rest of the trip jumping around in the car. Susan had said that ten hours was too long for her to have to ride on her first day, so Robin Hood's Purple Sandpiper and I spent Monday night at a motel in Schenectady. Unless you are a lifelong GE fan, there's not a lot to be said for Schenectady.

Robin Hood's Purple Sandpiper slept very little and was full awake at 5:10

Tuesday morning. We pulled out of Schenectady before dawn and got to Cambridge around noon. When we pulled into the driveway off Linnaean Street, Susan was sitting on the front steps of the big, five-colored painted-lady Victorian house where she lived and worked. As I got out of the car I said "Oh boy" to myself, which was what I always said, or some variation of that, whenever I saw her. Thick black hair, very big blue eyes, wide mouth, slim, in shape, great thighs, plus an indefinable hint of sensuality. She radiated a kind of excitement, the possibility of infinite promise. It wasn't just me. Most people seemed to feel that spending time with Susan would be an adventure.

"Omigod," Susan said when Robin Hood's Purple Sandpiper and I got out of the car.

Susan's yard was fenced. I opened the front gate and closed it behind us and unhooked the dog from her leash. She was uneasy.

Susan said, "Pearl."

The dog pricked her long ears a little. Then she ran around Susan's smallish front yard in a random way as if she were trying to find a point of stable reference. Finally she decided that I was her oldest friend outside Canada and came over to me and leaned in against my leg for emotional support.

Susan watched her with the full-focus concentration that made her such a good therapist. If she concentrated on something long enough, it would begin to smolder.

"Pearl?" Susan said.

The dog looked at her carefully and wagged her tail tentatively. Susan nodded slowly.

"She's back," Susan said.

"Yes," I said. "She just doesn't know it yet."

Susan crouched at the foot of her stairs and opened her arms.

"Pearl," she said again.

The dog walked to Susan and sniffed her. Susan put her cheek against the dog's muzzle and patted the dog's head.

"She'll know it soon," Susan said.

8

♦ ♦ ♦ ♦ ♦

I was in the lobby of the New Federal Courthouse on Fan Pier.

"International Consulting Bureau," I said.

I gave my card to the guard and he looked at it, then checked his computer screen.

"Whom do you wish to speak with there?"

"Whom?"

The guard looked up at me and grinned. "It's the training program they give us," he said.

"I wish to speak with Mr. Ives," I said.

He nodded, punched up a number, and spoke into the phone.

"Mr. Spenser to see Mr. Ives."

He nodded and hung up.

"Over there," he said, "through the metal detector, take the elevator to the fifteenth floor."

"There a room number?" I said.

"Someone will meet you at the elevator, sir."

"Of course," I said.

At the security barrier there were four guards from the Federal Protection Service.

"I have a gun on my right hip," I said to them. "I'm going to unclip it and hand it to you, holster and all."

The guards spread out slightly and two of them rested hands on their holstered guns. The head guard was a black man who looked like retired military.

"And do you have a permit, sir?"

"I do."

"First the gun, then the permit," he said.

I handed him the holstered gun, then I took my permit from my shirt pocket where I had put it in anticipation of this moment. The head guard read it carefully.

"We'll hang on to the gun and the permit," he said. "You can pick them up on the way out."

"You're asking me to risk the federal courthouse unarmed?" I said.

The guard's face stayed serious.

"Yes, sir," he said. "We are."

He swept his arm toward the metal detector, and I went through without incident.

"Elevators are there, sir."

"Stay alert," I said. "If I run into trouble, I'll scream."

"We'll be here, sir."

At the fifteenth floor there was a woman with long, silver hair and a severe young face. She was dressed in a black pantsuit and a mannish white shirt with a narrow black tie. Her black shoes had very high heels. We stepped into a long hallway. There were office doors along both sides of it. The hallway floor was carpeted in dark red. There was no identification on any of the office doors, all of which were closed.

"Spenser," I said.

"Follow me, please," she said.

There were discreet security cameras at either end of the hall. I smiled at the one I was facing. It's good to be cheery. The severe woman knocked on the last door on the right.

From inside, a voice said, "Come."

The woman opened the door and stepped aside, and I went in. Ives was sitting at an empty desk in a blank room with a view of the harbor. He looked at me without expression until the door closed and we were alone.

Then he smiled, sort of, and said, "Well, well, young Lochinvar."

"How about maturing Lochinvar," I said.

"You're as old as you feel," Ives said, and

gestured at the straight chair in front of his desk. "Sit."

Ives was sort of tall and leathery with sandy hair. He wore a tan poplin suit with a pink oxford button-down shirt and a pink bow tie with black polka dots. The room was entirely without ornamentation except for Ives's Yale diploma framed on the wall behind his desk.

"You ever hear of an antiestablishment organization in 1974 that called itself the Dread Scott Brigade?"

Ives smiled his dim smile. "It is my business to hear of things," he said. "Why do you ask?"

"They killed a woman in a bank holdup in Boston in September of 1974."

"And were never caught," Ives said.

I nodded.

"Which is why you're here," he said.

"Yes."

"You're going to catch them."

"I am."

"Except you don't know who they are."

"Not yet," I said.

"Or if they even exist," Ives said.

"Somebody killed her," I said.

"Why do you think it was this group?"

"Cops got a letter from them afterwards, claiming responsibility."

"Anyone can write a letter," Ives said.

"It's a place to start," I said.

"I suppose it is."

Ives folded his hands over his flat stomach and leaned back in his chair and rested one foot on the edge of his desk. He made a slight gesture with his lips, which I had decided to treat as a smile.

"So, you ever hear of them."

"They are a domestic group," Ives said. "We concern ourselves with international issues. Have you consulted our counterintelligence cousins at the Bureau?"

"There seems to be a missing file."

Ives smiled again. "Ahhh!" he said.

"Ahhh?"

Ives began to nod his head slowly as he spoke.

"How do you know it exists?" he said.

"It was mentioned in a police report. Said an FBI intelligence file was coming."

"And it wasn't there."

"No."

"And the FBI can't find it."

"No."

"What does that tell you?" he said.

"Two possibilities," I said.

"One being that they are sloppy filers," Ives said.

"And the other that something is being covered up."

Ives rocked in his chair for a moment. "While the terms FBI and Intelligence are oddly disparate," he said, "I have not found them to be sloppy filers."

We were both quiet. Below us the harbor was gray and choppy in the May sunshine. One of the water shuttle boats from Rowe's Wharf was trudging toward the airport.

"You're telling me something," I said.

"I am a member of a highly secretive government agency," Ives said. "We tell no one anything."

"Of course," I said.

9

◆ ◆ ◆ ◆ ◆

Hawk and I were running intervals on the red composite track in back of Harvard Stadium. The sun was shining. The temperature was about 65. I was wearing a cutoff sweatshirt that was black with sweat. Hawk seemed calm. We would do a couple 220s, a couple 440s, and a couple 880s, and then walk a 440. We were walking again.

"Maybe we should walk an extra two-twenty," I said.

"Ain't two-twenties anymore," Hawk said. "I keep telling you. They two hundred meters, four hundred meters, and eight hundred meters."

"How do you know?" I said.

"Ah is an African-American," Hawk said. "We know shit like that. You see a lot of European Americans running those races?"

"European Americans?" I said.

Hawk grinned.

"I can always tell," I said, "when you're sleeping with some theorist from one of the colleges."

"Abby," Hawk said. "She teach at Brandeis."

"I'll bet she does," I said.

"She a feminist, too," Hawk said.

"Of course she is," I said. "You want to walk another two-twenty?"

"Sure," Hawk said. "I know you need it."

"I was thinking of you," I said.

Some of the Harvard track kids flashed by us, running their own training sprints. I was glad we were walking. I had the feeling they'd have flashed past us even if we'd been running. Some of them were women.

"You ever hear of a group back in the seventies," I said, "called itself the Dread Scott Brigade?"

"Nope."

"Part of the radical movement," I said. "They held up a bank in Audubon Circle in 1974, killed a woman."

"I remember that," Hawk said. "I believe there was a brother in on it."

"Yes."

"Lotta brothers in radical movements then," Hawk said.

"Ungrateful bastards," I said. "We rescue their ancestors from ignorance, teach them to chop cotton. And that's the thanks we get?"

"Good works don't always get re-

44

warded," Hawk said, without any hint of a ghetto accent. His speech flowed in and out of Standard English for reasons known only to him. Most things about Hawk were known only to him.

"How come you weren't a radical?" I said.

"I was into crime?"

"Oh yeah."

"So how come you interested?"

I told him about Paul and Daryl and the missing FBI report. Then we ran some 220s and some 440s and some 880s. I kept up pretty well for a European American.

When we were walking again, Hawk said, "Quirk know about this missing report?"

"Uh-huh."

"And the FBI guy?"

"Epstein," I said. "Yeah, he knows."

"But neither one of them can find it."

"They haven't yet."

Both of us paused to watch a pair of young Harvard women jog past. As we watched them I said to Hawk, "You think staring at them is sexist behavior?"

"Yes," Hawk said.

I nodded.

"That's what I thought," I said.

Hawk was silent for maybe twenty yards. The Harvard women were halfway around the turn.

Then he said, "Quirk wants to find something, he usually do."

"Yes," I said.

"Don't know Epstein. But he don't get to be SAC 'cause he a good old Irish Catholic boy."

"No."

"So he might be pretty good, too."

"Be my guess," I said.

Hawk was wearing black satiny polyester running pants and a sleeveless mesh shirt. From the far turn the two Harvard women looked back at him.

"We think he good. We know Quirk be good," Hawk said. "So there a reason they don't find this report?"

I shrugged.

"Maybe there's a reason they can't look," I said.

"And maybe they hoping you'll do the looking for them."

"That occurred to me," I said.

Hawk looked at me for a minute. His expression was as unfathomable as it always was.

"Good," Hawk said.

10

Pearl lay at full length between Susan and me.

"It's odd," Susan said. "Being in bed with a strange dog."

"That describes my life before I met you," I said.

"Oh, oink!" Susan said.

"Sexism again?" I said.

"In the extreme," Susan said.

"You chicks are so sensitive," I said.

"You too, big guy," Susan said.

We were quiet, listening to the faint breathing sound Pearl made as she slept.

"I don't love her yet," Susan said. "Like I did the first Pearl."

"Not yet," I said.

"But we will," Susan said.

"Yes."

The room was nearly dark, lit faintly by the ambient illumination of the outside city.

"It's fascinating to see her beginning to morph into Pearl," Susan said.

"She's doing that," I said. "Isn't she."

"I know it's me, of course," Susan said. "I know she's not really changing."

"Maybe she is," I said.

"You think?"

"There are more things in this world than in all your philosophies, Horatio."

"I think you might have somewhat mangled the quote," Susan said.

"Is there a copy of Hamlet in the house?" I said.

"I don't think so."

"Then I stand by my quote," I said.

Pearl stood up and turned around several times and settled back down with her feet sticking into my stomach.

"You're lying on her side of the bed," Susan said.

"I prefer to think of it as her lying on my side."

"Well, at least she's the only one."

"Oh, good," I said.

"She does present something of an obstacle," Susan said.

"You feel that if I were to press my pulsating maleness upon you," I said, "she might react?"

"Pulsating maleness?"

"Throbbing masculinity?" I said.

"My God," Susan said. "And yes, I think she'd bark and snuffle and paw at us and probably try to become part of the festivities."

"And if we put her in another room?"

"She'll yowl," Susan said.

"We could pretend it's you," I said.

"We could run cold water on your pulsating maleness," Susan said.

"She's pretty used to the car," I said. "I could take her out and put her in it."

"Yes," Susan said. "That would work, I think."

"I could even give her a ride around the block so she'd think she actually was going someplace."

"Even better," Susan said.

"While I'm gone you could take off those pajamas," I said.

"I bought these pajamas for you."

"When I complained about the sweatpants?"

"Yes. They even had the word 'enticing' on the package," Susan said.

" 'Better than sweatpants' doesn't look as good on a label," I said.

I put on my pants and shoes and took Pearl on her short leash downstairs to the driveway. I let her jump into the backseat and drove once around the block and back into the driveway.

"I'll be back soon," I said.

And she fell for it.

11

◆ ◆ ◆ ◆ ◆

It wasn't quite a play Paul had written, nor exactly a dance that he'd choreographed, nor precisely an evening of cabaret, though it had all those elements. It was called "Poins." And it integrated Shakespearean characters, songs from 1950s musicals, and choreography which referenced both eras. I had always liked watching the kid perform, but over the years some of the things he'd performed in had made me tired. But that had been other people's stuff. Doing his own stuff, Paul was touching, smart, and funny. If I weren't so hard-bitten, I'd have been thrilled. When the play was over, Paul and Daryl came back to Susan's place to meet Pearl.

"My God," Paul said when Pearl got off the couch, came over carefully, and sniffed him with considerable reserve. "She's really beautiful."

Susan said, "Pearl, say hello to your brother, Paul."

Daryl looked a little cautious, and when Pearl sniffed her I could see her tense. This did not bode well.

"I have sandwiches," Susan said. "Let me set the table while you have a drink."

"We can eat at the counter," Paul said.

"No, no," Susan said. "It will only take me a minute."

Paul smiled at me. "Why did I say that?"

"Because you're a slow learner," I said. "You knew what the answer would be."

"Good china," Paul said. "And many glasses and two spoons each and linen napkins in napkin rings."

"Should I help?" Daryl said.

She was still alert to any false moves Pearl might make.

"No," Paul said.

Paul drank a couple beers in what appeared to be one continuous swallow. His performance had been exhaustingly physical, and even when it wasn't, it always took him some time to come down. I knew he'd be quiet for awhile.

"Does your aunt still live in Boston?" I said.

"She retired," Daryl said. "Someplace up in Maine."

"Have you seen her since you've been here?"

"No. We weren't really close after my mother died."

51

"So you went back to La Jolla."

"Yes."

"And lived with your father?"

"Yes."

"When did you start performing?"

She shrugged. "My mom used to take me to the children's program at the La Jolla Playhouse," she said. "Both my parents were very supportive. My mom and dad never missed anything I was in."

"Your father still in La Jolla?" I said.

"Yes," Daryl said. "I had an unusually wonderful childhood, before . . ." she made a little rolling gesture with her right hand. "We were a really close-knit family. We did everything together."

"Siblings?" I said.

"No. Just Mom, and Dad, and me."

"Where in Maine does your aunt live?"

"I don't know, a funny name. I think it's the place where that ex-president lives."

"George Bush?"

"Yes."

"Kennebunkport," I said.

"That sounds right."

Paul was watching me.

"What's your aunt's name?" I said.

"I think it's Sybil Pritchard now," Daryl said. "Why?"

"I thought maybe I'd talk with her," I said.

"I'd rather you didn't."

Paul was frowning a little.

"Okay," I said.

"And your father's name is Gordon," I said. "Like yours."

"Yes."

Susan came in wearing a small, clean apron that said BORN TO COOK across the front.

Paul looked at the apron and smiled. "That would be irony," Paul said, "right?"

"It would," Susan said. "Supper's ready."

There was a very big platter of finger sandwiches and composed salad plates with asparagus, cherry tomatoes, and artichoke hearts.

"My God, Susan," Daryl said. "You put this all together while we were having a drink?"

Susan smiled modestly.

"What kind of sandwiches are they?" Daryl said. She seemed a little uneasy about Pearl's nose resting on the edge of the table near her.

"Oh," Susan said, "a lovely assortment."

Paul looked at me and made a little sound that might have been a laugh, smothered.

"Are you laughing?" Daryl said. "I need to know what they are. There's a lot of stuff I can't eat."

"I'm not laughing at you," Paul said.

Susan said, "He's laughing at me, Daryl. I have never actually made a sandwich, I believe, in my entire life."

"So where'd you get these."

"I have a caterer friend who has a key," Susan said. "I called her on my cell phone."

It was in fact a lovely assortment: tuna, smoked salmon, egg salad, cheese, turkey, cucumber with Boursin, and corned beef. Daryl carefully examined the contents of each one before she selected from the platter. She ate two sandwiches, both turkey, and ate the cherry tomatoes from her salad.

We talked about the play. We complimented both of them. We had no further conversations about Daryl's aunt, whom she'd rather I not talk to, nor Daryl's childhood, which had been idyllic.

12

Hawk and I were in Codman Square in a coffee shop eating grilled English muffins. A tall, thin, hard-faced black guy with a gray Afro, wearing a white dress shirt buttoned to the neck, walked in and came to our table. Several people in the coffee shop looked at him covertly.

"Hawk," he said.

"Sawyer," Hawk said.

The black man sat down next to Hawk.

"The blue-eyed devil is Spenser," Hawk said. "Sawyer McCann, the last hippie."

We nodded at each other. Sawyer made no attempt to shake hands.

"You notice how out of place you look here," McCann said.

I was the only white person in the room. "I do," I said.

"That is how it feels for us, much of the time."

"I thought of that," I said.

"So how's it make you feel?" McCann said.

"Like clinging to Hawk, but I'm too proud."

Hawk grinned. McCann's face never changed.

"Well," he said. "At least you don't apologize for being white."

"Not my fault," I said.

"Sawyer know something about the Dread Scott Brigade," Hawk said.

I nodded and looked at McCann and waited. The waitress came and refilled our coffee cups and poured one for McCann. McCann stirred in six spoonfuls of sugar, pouring it from the old-fashioned glass container into his spoon to measure, and then into the coffee.

McCann sipped some of his coffee, watching me as he did.

"I might help you," he said. "But if I do, it's because Hawk ask me."

"Okay."

"I never met a white man I could trust," McCann said.

I waited.

"I never met one I liked."

I let that slide.

"I never met one wasn't a racist motherfucker," McCann said. "You a racist?"

Hawk watched quietly, his eyes bright with pleasant amusement.

"Not till now," I said.

McCann's tight face got tighter. "You fucking with me?" he said.

"I am," I said.

McCann sat back in the booth a little and put his coffee mug down. "You ain't scared of me," he said. "Are you."

"Nope."

"Most white people you get in their face they get scared."

"That's a racist reaction," I said.

Hawk didn't say anything, but there was still a hint of amusement around his eyes.

"I usually count on it," McCann said.

"Sorry," I said.

"Okay," McCann said.

He drank some more coffee.

" 'Bout 1972," he said. "They having a lotta problems between the black prisoners and the white prisoners in the various prison systems. So they invite a bunch of radical white kids from a bunch of, ah, liberal universities to come in and promote racial harmony. Workshops, seminars, that shit. You remember what it was like in 1972."

I nodded.

"And it don't work so well," McCann almost smiled. "Kids decide the black prisoners are victims of white racism and they

57

stir up more trouble than there was before."

"You think the kids were right?" I said.

McCann had decided to accept me, for
the moment at least, and most of the hard-
case manner had sloughed off, though it
hadn't been replaced by anything resem-
bling soft.

"Some of the brothers in jail were political prisoners," McCann said. "Still are.
Some of them were rapists and murderers
and thieves and bullies, and the kids'
problem was they couldn't tell which was
which."

"Because they were all black," I said.

"Uh-huh."

"Racism works in mysterious ways," I
said. "It's wonders to perform."

"So these kids decide to form the Dread
Scott Brigade, which a sort of loose national network to help victims of white fas-
cist oppression," McCann said. "Kind of
name college kids would think up. And
they going to work for the freedom of the
prisoners."

"How'd that go?" I said.

"Couple of the prisoners escaped. Don't
know if the kids helped them or not."

I waited. McCann looked thoughtful.
The waitress came by and filled our coffee

cups. I watched McCann go through his sugar-loading routine. He stirred carefully until he was sure all the sugar had dissolved into the coffee.

"One of the prisoners they working with was a brother name Abner Fancy."

"Abner Fancy," I said.

"He change it to Shaka in prison."

"Don't blame him," I said. "Did he stick with the Dread Scott Brigade?"

"Become the boss," McCann said.

"He shoot the woman in the bank holdup?" I said.

"Don't know."

"You know him?"

"Nope."

"But you heard about him."

"Yep."

"You got any other names?"

"Brother in there with him name Coyote."

"You know his, ah, slave name?"

"No."

"Know any of the white kids?"

"No."

"Know where any of these people are now?" I said.

"No."

"Cops ever talk to you about this?" I said.

59

"I don't talk to cops," McCann said.

We were silent for a moment.

"How come you never changed your name?" I said.

"Some of us be who we are," McCann said. "You see Jim Brown call himself Shaka?"

"No," I said.

"Everybody get named by somebody," McCann said. "My father named me."

"Funny," I said. "That's what happened to me."

We all drank our coffee. My English muffin was gone. Did I want another one.

"Lemme ask you," McCann said to me. "I decided to come upside your head, you think anyone in here would help you?"

I decided I did want another English muffin, but I wouldn't have one because it would be self-indulgent, and Susan might find out.

"Two answers," I said to McCann. "One, I wouldn't need any help. And, two, he would."

I gestured toward Hawk with my head. McCann shifted his stare onto him.

"You do that?"

"Two answers," Hawk said. "One, I would. And two, I wouldn't need to."

"Why do you ask?" I said.

"Just getting the lay of the land," McCann said.

"Well that's how it lays," I said. "Thanks for your help."

McCann finished his coffee, put the cup down very carefully on the table, nodded at Hawk, stood, and walked away.

"Effervescent," I said.

Hawk smiled. "Sawyer a little stern," he said.

"He is," I said.

13
◆ ◆ ◆ ◆ ◆

The theater was dark on Mondays, and I took Paul to dinner at the world's greatest restaurant, which is, of course, The Agawam Diner in Rowley. The place was always crowded for breakfast and lunch, but on a Monday evening, early, it was not busy and we got a nice booth with a view of the traffic light at the Route 133 intersection.

"Are you and Daryl an item?" I said.

"God no," Paul said. "I like her, but she's way too crazy for me."

"Crazy how?" I said.

"She drinks too much. She smokes dope too much. She sleeps around too much. She's too intense about her career."

"What do you know about her family?" I said.

"Nothing," Paul said. "Except for her mother's murder she never talks about her family, except that it was a close-knit loving family. Like the other night."

"So she didn't talk specifically about her mother?"

"Just about the murder. The murder is

very big in her life."

The waitress brought us menus.

"My God," he said. "Actual food."

"No reduction of kiwi," I said.

"No skate wings," Paul said. "No pâté of Alsatian bluebird. No caramelized parsnip puree with fresh figs."

The waitress took our order.

"Why do you suppose she didn't want me to talk with her aunt?"

"Daryl's hard to understand," Paul said.

"She ever talk about her father?" I said.

"No. I always sort of assumed he was dead."

"Siblings?" I said.

"She never mentioned any."

"How long have you known her?"

"Two years," Paul said. "We worked together in the first play I did in Chicago. When she's up, she's a hell of a lot of fun."

The waitress brought smothered pork chops for Paul, spaghetti and meatballs for me.

"Why are you asking about her?"

"Because I don't know about her."

Paul was nodding as I spoke.

"And that's what you do," he said. "You ask unanswered questions."

"Information is good," I said.

"So how come you didn't ask more

about the aunt?"

I smiled.

"Because you're going to go up to Maine and see her," Paul said. "You have her name and the town she lives in."

My mouth was full of spaghetti. I nodded. I was eying the assortment of pies behind the counter as I ate. Plan ahead.

"I know another reason you asked if she were my girlfriend," Paul said.

"Paternal solicitude," I said.

"Besides that," Paul said. "If she were my girlfriend, then you'd have to welcome her to the family. And she's afraid of dogs."

"Not a trait I value," I said.

I eyed the pies again. I thought one of them might be cherry.

"Of course we're not exactly family," Paul said.

"Depends on how you define family," I said.

"You, Susan, and me?"

I nodded.

"And Pearl?" he said.

"Of course," I said.

"How about Uncle Hawk?"

"Uncle Hawk?"

"Uh-huh."

"I think Uncle Hawk is all the family Uncle Hawk needs," I said.

14

In Kennebunkport, Sybil Pritchard lived in a small house with an oblique view of the water. She had shoulder-length gray hair and bare feet and wore a floral-patterned blue-and-yellow ankle-length dress.

"Well," she said when she answered the door. "You're a big strapping boy, aren't you."

"I am," I said. "Could we talk for a bit? About your sister's murder?"

"My sister was murdered thirty years ago," she said.

"Twenty-eight," I said. "Can we talk?"

"Are you a policeman?" she said.

"I'm a private detective, working for your niece."

"Daryl?" she said. "Come in. Sit down. Tell me what you want."

Her house was coastal cute, with a hemp rug, lobster pot coffee tables, steering-wheel mirrors, ship's captain lamps, and big scallop-shell ashtrays. There were a lot of butts in the ashtrays, and when we sat in her front room, Sybil immediately lit another cigarette and didn't apologize. There was a big Shaker table in front of a bay window where you could see a scrap of the ocean. On it were several spiral-bound notebooks and a blue champagne flute with pencils in it. She saw me look.

"I write poetry," she said. "By hand. The tactile sensation of actual transcription seems vital to the creative process."

I nodded.

"What can you tell me about your sister's death?" I said.

"Nothing. She was in a bank. Some radicals held it up. One of them shot her."

"Where were you at the time."

"Movies. I took Daryl to see *Harry and Tonto.*"

"Your sister was in Boston to visit you," I said.

"She was crashing with me," Sybil said. "She was in Boston chasing some guy."

Sybil's face was dark from sun and tough from wind and deeply lined from maybe too many cigarettes. She was about sixty, and she sat with her legs apart, one arm tucking the slack dress between her legs.

"Who?" I said.

"Don't know. She was always chasing some guy, dragging the damn kid along," Sybil said.

66

She took in smoke and exhaled slowly. I quit smoking in 1963. The smell no longer pleased me.

"How about her husband?"

"Poor Barry," Sybil said. "He married her, when she got pregnant with Daryl, you know, sort of do the right thing?"

"Were they married long?"

"Hell, I don't really know who married them. You know? They may have just sworn an oath of flower power."

"They were hippies?"

"Sure. Me too."

"Drugs?"

"You better believe it," Sybil said.

"Pot?"

"Everything," she said. "If I could light it on fire I'd smoke it."

"Been off for awhile?"

"I quit in March of 1978," she said.

She snuffed out her cigarette butt, took a fresh one from its pack and lit it, and took a long drag.

"Except for these," she said. "I coulda lit this one from the other one. But I hate the chain-smoke image. So I always put one out before I light another one."

"I admire self-control," I told her.

"You probably quit years ago."

"I did."

"You don't have any of that sunken-cheeks look," she said. "Like me."

I had nothing to say about that, so I cleverly looked around the room. There were some genuinely awful seascapes framed on the walls.

"Were they together long?" I said. "After Daryl was born?"

"Emily and Barry? Depends what you mean by together. You know how we all were then?"

"I recall the period," I said.

"Yes, of course you do. You were probably off somewhere doing push-ups. A lot of us were crazy to be unconventional. If older people did it, we couldn't possibly do it. My father was in the Rotary Club, for God's sake. My mother played fucking bridge!"

"So what about Barry and Emily?"

"Emily would go off and have an interlude with some guy who looked like Rasputin, and when he dumped her she'd come back to Barry."

"And Barry took her back."

"He didn't want to look conventional, I think. You know? Never darken my door again? I was in a pretty long-term fog during the time."

"And they lived in La Jolla?"

"La Jolla?" Sybil laughed. It was an unpleasant guttural. "My father and mother lived in La Jolla. Emily and Barry lived under a Coronado Bridge ramp." She laughed the guttural laugh again. "La Jolla!"

"After Emily's death, Daryl went back to her father?"

"Yes."

"And when's the last time you saw her?"

"That was it," Sybil said. "I guess Barry didn't feel very good about the Gold girls."

"That was your maiden name?"

"Yep. Gold."

Sybil started on her third cigarette.

"Is there a Mr. Pritchard?"

"And before that a Mr. Halleck and a Mr. Layne and a Mr. Selfridge. After Pritchard, I stopped marrying them."

"You have any idea who might have killed your sister?"

"One of the hippies in the bank," she said. "Nobody knows which one."

"Just for the hell of it," I said.

"That's what the cops told me," she said.

"Any reason to doubt it?"

"Nope."

"Any idea who the hippies are?"

"Nope."

"Or where?"

"Nope."

"How about the guy she was in Boston chasing? Any thoughts on him?"

"He was probably a jerk," Sybil said. "It's what she went after."

"Any special kind of jerkiness?"

"She liked the blowhard revolutionaries, mostly. You know, a lot of hair? Power to the people? Got any dope?"

"And you're out of that life now?"

She smiled. "Got awful hard being a hippie by 1980 or so."

"Was probably never easy," I said.

"You got that right — constant worry that you might turn into your mother. Had to stay alert all the time."

"And you've not had any contact with Daryl all that time?"

"I send her a card every Mother's Day. I'm not sure why. I do them myself. I'm a painter." She nodded at the execrable seascapes. "I did all of those."

"Splendid," I said.

"I do enjoy my poetry. But it's not as good — yet. My real talent is painting."

I took a card out and gave it to her.

"If anything occurs to you, please let me know," I said.

"Sure," she said and went to her Shaker table and tucked the card under the blotter. Then she went to a short, narrow bookcase and took out a slim volume of computer printouts. There were several others left on the shelf.

"Take a copy of my poetry with you," she said. "I think you might enjoy it."

"Thank you," I said.

On the way back to Boston, I stopped in Kittery for a sandwich and a cup of coffee. While I ate, I read some of Sybil's poems, and when I departed, I left them in the trash can along with the empty coffee cup and the wrapper from the sandwich.

15

It was late, and I needed to think. I bought a bottle of Scotch at a New Hampshire liquor store on my way down from Maine, and a submarine sandwich in Saugus. I was carrying both when I left my car in the alley and went up to my office.

The back stairwell was ugly in the nasty brightness of the fluorescent lights, and so was the hall. The black lettered sign on my office door told the world that I was a private investigator, or at least the part of the world that walked along this hall. I stuck the bottle under my left arm and got out my keys and opened my door.

There was a sweet chemical smell in my office. It wasn't very strong, but it was there. It was a smell I knew. Susan, getting ready to go out. Hairspray! I left the keys in the lock and stepped into my office sideways to keep from silhouetting myself in the open doorway. The Scotch remained under my left arm. The sub sandwich was in my left hand. My gun was out. Nothing moved. There was a little light spilling in from the hall and a little less light drifting up through my window from Berkeley Street.

As my pupils dilated, I could see someone sitting behind my desk. I had a vague sense of a presence on the wall to my right.

"On the left side of the kneehole under the desk," I said. "There's a switch, controls the overhead."

I narrowed my eyes against the light. Nothing happened. No one moved.

"I would rather not shoot you in the dark," I said.

Another moment when nothing stirred. Then a movement. And the lights came on.

There were two men: the guy at my desk and another man standing against the wall just to the right of the bay window. Neither one was showing a weapon. I kept mine in hand, but let it hang by my side.

"You have a bottle of Scotch whisky," the guy at my desk said.

"I do," I said. "And I'm willing to share. But the sandwich is mine."

The guy at my desk had a lot of teeth and very large black-rimmed glasses. His elbows rested on the arms of my chair. He had pale hands and long fingers, which he tented in front of his chin. His hair was smooth, flat to his head, and shiny black. Hairspray.

"The Scotch will suffice," he said. "You have glasses, or must we pass it around like three winos." His voice had an undertone to it, like the murmur of machinery deep in the ground.

"I have the setups," I said.

The guy standing against the wall was round-looking, with a red face and a thick blond mustache that twirled up at either end. Both men remained still while I put the Scotch and the sub sandwich on the desktop, and my gun back into its holster. I got some ice from the little office refrigerator, and glasses and soda from the glass-front cherry cabinet that Susan had installed, which went with the rest of my décor like a necklace on a toad. I put it all on the desk in front of Pale Fingers and sat down in a client chair.

"One of you can mix," I said. "Scotch and soda, a lot of ice, a lot of soda."

I unwrapped my sandwich while the blond guy made the drinks. The guy at my desk had his with soda, no ice. The blond guy had it on the rocks, not many rocks. He handed me mine and went back and stood against the wall. I had a bite of my sub and a slug of my Scotch and soda, and waited.

The guy at my desk took his time with the whisky, sipping it gently, letting it sit a moment in his mouth before swallowing it delicately.

"Good year for Scotch," I said.

He smiled at me aimlessly. The blond guy took about half of his Scotch at the first pull.

"I'm with the government," the guy at my desk said. "We both are."

"How nice for the government," I said.

"You weren't here," he said. "We took the liberty."

"It's a way to get shot," I said.

"What gave us away?" he said.

"Hairspray," I said.

"You smelled it."

"Yep."

"Vanity will be my downfall," he said.

I took another bite of my sandwich, trying to keep the peripheral fallout off my shirt. I chewed. I swallowed. I had a drink of Scotch.

"Whaddya want?" I said.

Pale Fingers nodded and smiled.

"Direct," he said. "I like that."

I had another bite of my sandwich and waited.

"We are here to ask a favor of you, in the interest of security."

I sipped some Scotch.

"You have been asking questions about the death of a woman named Emily Gordon."

The blond guy with the mustache looked at me steadily. I think he was being menacing.

"We would prefer that you desist."

"Because?"

"Because it is in the best interest of the United States."

"How so?" I said.

"I'm sorry," he said. "I'm afraid I can't share that with you."

"What a shame."

"And if that is unpersuasive," he said, "I might suggest that it would be very much in your best interest as well."

I finished my sub. It was excellent. But that was true of almost all subs.

"Agreed?" Pale Fingers said.

I finished the rest of my drink.

"Buzz off," I said.

The guy at my desk was tenting his fingers again. He glanced at the blond guy. The blond guy was still giving me the hard eye.

"Are you sure you want to provoke the

animosity of your government?" Pale Fingers said.

His mouth was tight and his eyes, even magnified by his glasses, looked very small.

"If this be treason," I said, "let us make the most of it."

"Unless you reconsider," Pale Fingers said, "we may find reason to investigate you."

"Given your track record," I said, "I remain undaunted."

"And a tax audit is not impossible."

"Yikes," I said.

Pale Fingers and the blond guy looked at each other. Pale Fingers shrugged. The blond guy shrugged back. Pale Fingers stood.

"You'll hear from us again," he said.

"Oh good," I said. "I hate when friendships sour."

We all looked at each other for a moment. None of us seemed scared. When they left, I made myself a fresh drink and went around behind my desk and reclaimed my chair. I put my feet up and looked at the open door into the bright, empty hallway, and thought.

16

◆ ◆ ◆ ◆ ◆

I met Epstein for breakfast in a coffee shop near his office. He was there when I arrived, sitting at a table, drinking coffee.

"Get a couple of these inside you and the day looks better," he said.

A waitress brought me orange juice and coffee. I drank the juice, put cream and sugar in my coffee, stirred, and had a sip. Epstein was right. Orange juice and coffee never let you down.

"This conversation going to be long enough so we should eat?" I said.

"We'd be fools not to," Epstein said.

I had a raspberry scone. Epstein had two eggs sunny-side up, bacon, home fries, and a bagel.

"Maintaining the old cholesterol?" I said.

"Except for the bagel," Epstein said. "The bagel's a gesture toward my heritage."

"On that basis, I should have had the potatoes," I said.

"You want to know why I offered to buy

you breakfast?" Epstein said.

"I figured you wanted some law enforcement tips."

"That too," Epstein said. "But I been thinking about your old murder case."

"Emily Gordon," I said.

"Yes. I was thinking it might help matters a little if you knew the name of the agent in charge of the investigation."

"There was an investigation?"

"Well, we normally look into bank robberies."

My scone had a light brush of frosting on the top, which seemed to me an excellent touch.

"So who looked into this one," I said.

"Of course," Epstein said, "I am not at liberty to give you his name."

"Of course," I said.

"On the other hand, if you were to bribe me by paying for breakfast, simple courtesy would mandate some sort of response."

"Breakfast is on me," I said.

"Agent's name is Evan Malone."

"He still around?"

"He's retired," Epstein said.

"You know where he is?"

"Of course."

"What do I do for his address."

"I may need a second bagel," Epstein said.

"Jesus, you're hard," I said. "No wonder you got to be SAC."

"Do I get the bagel?" Epstein said.

"Yes."

"Malone's on a lake in New Hampshire. I took the liberty of writing it out for you."

"You knew I'd cave on the second bagel, didn't you?"

Epstein smiled. I took the address and put it in my shirt pocket.

"I'm willing to go as high as a dozen bagels," I said. "But I need to ask you a question."

Epstein nodded gravely and spread his hands in a welcoming gesture.

"You send a couple of employees around to talk with me last night?"

Epstein frowned.

"Employees?"

"Geeky-looking guy with big, round glasses and a lot of teeth," I said. "Blond guy, heavyset, big mustache."

"Employees," Epstein said.

"That's what they told me."

"They said they were with the Bureau?"

"Government," I said. "I inferred Bureau."

"Inferred? What kind of talk is that for a guy your size?"

"Large, but literate," I said. "They yours?"

Epstein shook his head. "Not mine," he said. "What did they want?"

"For me to leave Emily Gordon alone."

"The thirty-year-old murder."

"Twenty-eight."

Epstein nodded and looked around for the waitress. When he caught her eye, he gestured for more coffee. She came and poured some for both of us.

"Could I have another bagel?" Epstein said to her. "Toasted, with a shmeer?"

"You want that with cream cheese?" she said.

Epstein smiled. "Yes."

The waitress hurried off.

Epstein said, "They show you any ID?"

"No."

"So you don't know they were government?"

"No."

"But we know they were somebody, and somebody doesn't want you investigating the death of Emily Gordon."

"Or the whole case," I said. "It may not be Emily Gordon per se."

"Could be," Epstein said. "Could be the fear that if you investigate Emily Gordon, you'll find out something else."

"Or expose the cover-up."

"Or both," Epstein said. "Remember Watergate?"

"It wasn't the crime, it was the cover-up?" I said.

"Per se," Epstein said.

17

It was Sunday morning. Susan and I were walking Pearl II along the Commonwealth Avenue Mall toward Kenmore Square. She was still a little nervous in the city and tended to press in against Susan's leg when cars passed. I didn't blame her. If you were going to press a leg, Susan's would be an excellent choice.

"So," I said. "Daryl's idyllic La Jolla childhood appears to be, ah, exaggerated."

"Poor kid," Susan said.

"Why the false history?" I said.

"I imagine the real history is too painful," Susan said. "And if you need to, you can pretend so hard that it's almost true."

Traffic was sparse for the moment, and Pearl felt daring. She pulled vigorously on the leash in the direction of some pigeons.

"You think she believes it is true?" I said.

"No, she knows it's not," Susan said. "But it could have been. And she probably believes she's the kind of person that such a childhood would have produced."

"It's almost true, because it could have

been true," I said.

"And because it is the best way to explain the kind of person you are."

A motorcycle went past us toward the common. Pearl shrunk in on herself, tucked her tail down, got low, and pressed against Susan. Susan patted her.

"You'll get used to it," Susan said. "You'll be a city girl soon."

We crossed Exeter Street.

"You think I should tell Paul," I said.

"Does he need to know?"

"As far as I can tell, he's not planning to stroll into the sunset with her."

"Would it do him any good to know?"

"Probably make life harder," I said. "Having the secret, deciding whether to tell her he knows, thinking about the lie when he's trying to direct her in a play."

"So why tell him?"

"Because otherwise, I'll be keeping a secret from him."

Susan smiled. Pearl had recovered from the motorcycle and was stalking a trash barrel.

"Only you," Susan said, "would worry about such a thing."

"You wouldn't tell him?"

"I would be perfectly comfortable doing what I thought was in his best interest."

84

I nodded.

"I'll think about it," I said.

"I know you will," Susan said and bumped her head against my shoulder.

We pulled Pearl away from the trash barrel and went on across Fairfield.

"Did she think I wouldn't find out?" I said. "When she asked me for help?"

"Maybe she thought you would," Susan said.

18

◆ ◆ ◆ ◆ ◆

"How much does it mean to you that I find out who murdered Daryl's mother?" I said to Paul.

We were up an alley off Broad Street, drinking Irish whisky in a saloon called Holly's where I had once, for a couple months in my early youth, between fights, been a bouncer. The place looked the same, and I still liked to go there even though no one I knew then worked in Holly's now.

"What kind of question is that?" Paul said.

"Are you being disrespectful?" I said.

"I would say so, yes."

"Good."

"So why are you asking me about Daryl and her mother?" Paul said.

"I talked to her aunt the other day."

"The one she said you shouldn't talk to," Paul said.

"Yes, that one."

"And?"

"And now I know why she didn't want

me to talk with her."

Paul sipped a little Irish whisky. He held the glass up a little and looked at the ice and whisky against the light from behind the bar.

"Good stuff," he said.

"Perfect for male-bonding moments," I said.

"Are we having one?"

"Absolutely."

He nodded. The bar was long and narrow with a tin ceiling and wood paneling, which had darkened with age. The bottles arranged in front of the mirror behind the bar were a shimmer of color in the dim room.

"What did Auntie tell you?" he said.

"Daryl sort of reinvented her childhood," I said.

"Wish I could," he said. "How'd she do it?"

I told him.

When I got through, Paul said, "Wow. She's even more fucked up than I thought she was."

"My diagnosis," I said.

"She's a good actress, though," Paul said. "And I like her."

I nodded.

"So, what's the downside," Paul said, "to

you finding out who killed her mother."

"Besides me working my ass off for no money?"

"Besides that."

"I can't trust what she tells me," I said.

"Can you ever?"

"Mostly no," I said. "I also might find out a lot more than Daryl wants me to."

"You might," Paul said.

We both finished our whisky. The bartender brought two more. Paul didn't touch his for the moment. He stared into it. The afternoon had moved on, and the after-work guys who got off at four were coming in.

"When I first met you," Paul said after a time, "if you had done what I wanted you to do, where would I be now?"

"You got a lotta stuff in you," I said. "You might have turned it around on your own."

"You think that was likely?"

"No."

"Me either. This is going to fuck her up all her life," Paul said, "if it doesn't get cleaned up."

"Ah cursed spite that I'm the one to set it right," I said.

"Hamlet?" Paul said. "Sort of?"

"I think so."

We each rolled a small swallow of whisky

down our throats and let the warm illusion spread through us.

"You want me to chase this down," I said.

"All the way to the end."

"It's better to know than not know?"

"Much," Paul said.

19

♦ ♦ ♦ ♦ ♦

The man came into my office without knocking. I was working at my desk and didn't look up until I had finished snipping an "Arlo and Janis" from *The Globe* to post on Susan's refrigerator door. When I did look up, the man had closed the door behind him and was pointing a gun at my head.

"Arlo and Janis is one of my favorites," I said.

"You see the gun?" the man said.

"I do," I said. "Right there at the end of your arm."

"Boss wanted you to see the gun."

On the left-hand wall of my office was a leather couch. At either end was a brass floor lamp with a small brass shade over the lightbulb. The man glanced at it and casually put a bullet through the shade nearest me. The explosion filled the office and made my ears hurt. If the man's ears hurt, he didn't show it.

"Boss wanted you to see me shoot," he said.

The bullet had torn the small brass

shade apart, and it hung in twisted shards around the shattered lightbulb.

"Don't feel bad," I said. "That's the way I shot while I was learning."

The man let the gun hang by his right side. He was tall and languid, with longish blond hair, a deep tan, pale blue eyes, and a diamond stud in his left ear. He wore tan slacks, a double-breasted blue blazer, and a white shirt with a big collar that spilled out over his lapels. He had on light tan woven leather loafers and no socks. He smiled. It made his mouth thin and oddly turned the corners of his mouth down slightly. It was the kind of smile a shark would smile, if sharks smiled.

"I asked around about you," he said. "Everyone told me you were a funny guy."

I ducked my head modestly.

"What I want to know is how funny you'll be when you got a gut full of lead."

"A gut full of lead?" I said. "That's pathetic. Nobody talks like that anymore. A gut full of lead?"

"I don't think you're a funny guy," the man said. "And my boss don't think so. You need to stay away from the Emily Gordon case."

"You're not with the government, are you?" I said.

He paid no attention to me. The man really didn't think I was funny. He didn't think I was anything. The gun at his side was a 9mm Browning. I owned one just like it. He brought it up slowly and held it at arm's length, pointing it at my forehead. The hammer was back from the previous shot. He wasn't smiling, but there was still something shark-like in his face.

"You unnerstand what I tole you," he said.

"I think so," I said. "Who's your boss?"

He didn't say anything. The black bottomless barrel of the gun stared unwaveringly at my forehead.

"Okay," I said. "Be that way."

"I could do it now," he said.

His breathing seemed shallow and fast.

"You could, but you won't."

I focused on his trigger finger. If it showed any sign of movement I would roll to my right behind my desk and go for my gun. Except I wouldn't get behind my desk. He'd blow my head open while I was still in my chair. We both knew that. But I focused anyway. It was better than wondering if there was an afterlife.

"Why won't I?"

"You're supposed to scare me," I said.

"You scared?"

"Sure," I said. "But a lot of people know I'm working on Emily Gordon. You kill me and it will make the case hot again. Your boss knows that."

"Don't mean I won't kill you," he said.

His eyes seemed wider and a little unfocused.

"No, it don't," I said. "But it means you won't kill me now."

"You keep pushing on the Gordon thing," the man said, "and we won't have no reason to wait."

"Of course I might kill you," I said.

He licked his lips and there were faint smudges of color over his cheekbones.

"Pal," he said, "if there's a next time, you'll be dead before you see me."

"Does it hurt when they pierce your ears?" I said.

He stared at me over the gun.

"You know, when they put that cute diamond in your ear, was it painful?"

He stared at me some more.

Then he said, "Fuck you, pal," and walked out, still holding the gun.

20

I sat with Hawk and Vinnie Morris on a bench in Quincy Market, where we could keep track of the young female tourists. We had coffee in big paper cups. Vinnie had a jelly donut.

Hawk shook his head slowly.

"Don't know anybody sounds like your man," he said. "Like the diamond earring, though. You sure he's white?"

"Whiter than Christmas," I said. "Vinnie?"

Vinnie leaned forward a little so he wouldn't get jelly on his shirt.

"Vinnie," I said, "jelly donuts are the single uncoolest thing a man can eat."

"I like them," Vinnie said.

"Honkie soul food," Hawk said.

"You know anybody sounds like the guy I described?" I said to Vinnie.

"Yeah."

"So why didn't you say so?"

"I'm eating my donut," Vinnie said.

I looked at Hawk. Hawk grinned.

"Vinnie got a lotta focus," Hawk said.

Vinnie finished his donut and drank

some coffee. There was no sense of hurry, but all his movements were very quick. And exact. He patted his mouth with a paper napkin.

"Sounds to me like a guy named Harvey," he said.

"First name or last?"

"Don't know. He's from Miami," Vinnie said. "Comes up here sometimes, does gun work for Sonny Karnofsky."

"You know him?"

"I met him."

"How?"

Vinnie looked at me.

"I mean 'how?' in general," I said.

"I'm still with Gino," Vinnie said. "Him and Sonny was doing something. Harvey was walking behind Sonny."

"He any good?" I said.

"Yes."

"Better than you?" Hawk said.

"No," Vinnie said.

"As good as you?" I said.

"No."

Hawk grinned.

"Anybody good as you?" he said.

"Maybe that Mex from L.A."

"Chollo," I said.

"He's pretty good," Vinnie said.

Hawk looked at me. "Sonny took over

what Joe Broz left behind," Hawk said.

"Which is pretty much everything," I said.

"Except for Gino," Vinnie said.

"And Tony Marcus," Hawk said.

"Talk to me a little more about Harvey," I said.

Vinnie watched a youngish woman walk by in shorts and a cropped tank top. "Fucking broads got no shame," Vinnie said.

"It's one of the many things I like about them," Hawk said.

"Talk about Harvey," I said.

"He's good, but he's got no soul," Vinnie said. "He'll shoot anything."

"He like it?" I said.

"Yeah."

"Could he be working for anybody else?" I said.

"Up here? No. You work here for Sonny, you don't work for anybody else."

"You ever work for Sonny?" I said to Hawk.

"I don't like him," Hawk said.

"Is that a no?"

"It is."

"So why is Sonny Karnofsky worried about a counterculture murder that went down twenty-eight years ago?" I said.

"We criminals," Hawk said. "We don't know stuff like that."

"I don't either," I said. "I guess I'll have to talk with Sonny."

"That would suggest to him that you ain't leaving the case alone."

"It would," I said.

Hawk nodded. "I'll come along," he said.

"When we going to do it," Vinnie said.

"No reason to wait," I said.

21

Sonny Karnofsky practiced his profession out of the Pulaski Social Club, near the Charlestown line, a couple blocks into Somerville from Sullivan Square. It was a narrow three-decker with clapboard siding, faced on the first floor with rust-colored artificial stone. There was a large plate glass window to the right of the narrow entry door. Across the window, PULASKI SOCIAL CLUB was lettered in black. An unlaundered curtain hung across the inside of the window so you couldn't see in.

Vinnie waited in the car at the curb. Hawk got out with me and leaned against the car while I got out and walked to the club. There were a couple guys hanging outside the doorway, smoking cigarettes and drinking beer from the bottle and looking dangerous in the way only bottom-rung wiseguys were able to look while they waited for someone to tell them to do something. I started in the door, and a fat guy with a lot of tattoos put his arm out.

"You going somewhere?"

"Am I going somewhere," I said. "I never think of saying stuff like that until it's too late. That's great: Are you going somewhere. Hot dog!"

"What are you, a wiseguy?" the fat guy said.

"I am," I said. "And I'm looking for Sonny Karnofsky."

"Yeah?"

"I'm here to talk with him about Harvey."

The fat guy was getting a little careful. Maybe I was important.

"He know you're coming?"

"Tell him I'm here," I said.

The fat guy hesitated. He looked at Hawk leaning on the car. He looked at the other guy, much smaller, wearing a dirty tank top hanging outside pink Bermuda shorts, and black sandals.

"Find out if Sonny wants to see this guy," the fat guy said.

The guy in the sandals went inside. The fat man had dropped his arm, but stood with his body shielding the entrance. If I wasn't supposed to go in and he let me, Sonny would have his ass. If I was supposed to go in and he didn't let me, Sonny would have his ass. We waited. Hawk seemed to be enjoying it. Vinnie didn't seem to know it was happening. The other guy came back out.

"Okay," he said to the fat guy.

The fat guy turned to me.

"Okay," he said.

"I love a chain of command," I said.

The fat guy jerked his head toward the door, and the guy in the sandals opened it for me and I went in. There was a big shabby open room with a table and an old refrigerator against the wall to my right. Four guys were playing cards. Two other guys were at another table, drinking beer and watching *The Young and the Restless* on television. A big poster of the New England Patriots Super Bowl team was taped to the wall to my left. And straight ahead, to the left of a half-open door, was a large calendar with the days crossed off.

"Through that door in the back," the guy in the sandals told me.

As I walked through the room, the men stared at me. Probably sick with envy. Through the open door was the quintessential back room: dirty brown walls, brown linoleum floor, dirty window covered with wire mesh that looked out at the back of the next building. Old oak desk, old oak file cabinet, old cane-back oak swivel chair behind the desk, big old sagging armchair covered in shabby brown corduroy. In the armchair, crossways, with his legs swung over one of the chair arms, sat my recent acquaintance Harvey, wearing a white linen suit. In the old swivel chair like an imposing toad, wearing a red-and-blue Hawaiian shirt that gapped between the buttons over his stomach, was Sonny Karnofsky.

Sonny looked at me without expression. Harvey swung his leg sort of indolently and smirked a little. Sonny waited.

"You know me?" I said.

"Yeah."

"Why'd you send this fop around to scare me to death."

"What's a fop?" Sonny said.

I pointed at Harvey. With his white suit, he was wearing a pale blue shirt and a white tie. Flawless.

"What makes you think I sent him to do anything?"

"Oh come on, Sonny," I said. "You think he felt like threatening somebody, and he picked me out of the phone book? What I want to know is why you care about the murder of some woman from California, happened twenty-eight years ago?"

"Corkie says you got some people waiting for you outside," Sonny said.

There was maybe the hint of an Eastern European accent in his speech, but it was so faint that maybe it wasn't there.

"I do."

Sonny nodded slowly. "Good idea," he said.

His voice was thick, as if his pipes were clogged.

"Were you a counterculture radical in 1974?" I said.

He raised a hand and pointed at me with a forefinger so fat it made the skin taut.

"Anybody knows me will tell you, you fuck with me and you're dead."

"I've heard that," I said.

"And they'll tell you, fuck with my family and you'll wish you fucked with me."

"Family?"

Sonny was so used to being king of the hill these days that he probably didn't watch what he said as much as he used to. His face was expressionless, but his mouth clamped hard shut. We looked at each other for a moment. Without taking his eyes off me, he spoke to Harvey.

"Not here. But as quick as you can someplace else," Sonny said. "Kill him."

Harvey looked like a guy with a low-grade fever.

"Be my pleasure," Harvey said.

That pretty well said it all, so I turned and marched out. I hate to be in a place where I'm not wanted.

22

Sitting in my office, Daryl was sort of hunched with her hands in her lap.

"I never really think of it as lying," she said.

I nodded. Nondirective.

"It's . . ." she looked at Paul, who sat quietly next to her, even more nondirective, if possible, than I was. "It's more, like, how it should have been. You know? How it could have been, if my parents . . ."

"Sure," I said.

Paul and I looked supportively at Daryl. Daryl looked at her hands.

"They embarrassed me," she said.

"Your parents."

"Yes."

"Because?"

"Because? Because they were fucking hippies, for God's sake. Were your parents hippies?"

I thought of my father and my two uncles.

"No," I said. "They weren't."

"Most people's weren't. And even if they were, they got over it."

"They were different times," I said, just to say something.

"I'm lucky they didn't name me Moonflower."

"You are," I said.

Paul smiled. It was as if Daryl didn't hear me.

"We didn't come here to visit my aunt," Daryl said. "We came here with some man my mother was fucking."

Paul and I looked at each other. We were thinking of Paul's mother.

I had swiveled my chair a little so I could see out my window. Although it was early afternoon, the sky outside my office was dark and getting darker. Rain was coming. Daryl sat without saying anything.

"Your father know about this man?"

"I don't know what he knew," Daryl said. "I think he was stoned for the first twelve years of my life."

"Were they separated?" I said.

She didn't answer for awhile. She had stopped looking at her lap and begun to look out through my window at the rain that hadn't come yet. I was about to ask again when she answered me.

"Separated?" she laughed. "Hell, I don't

know if they were even married. I mean, maybe some long-haired freak in a tie-dyed shirt mumbled something and smoked hemp with them. But separated? From what?"

"Did your father know your mother, ah, fooled around?"

"Oh, yes."

"Did he object?"

"Maybe when he wasn't stoned. But she didn't care. She wasn't going to be somebody's chattel."

"Right on, sister," I said. "Your father fool around?"

"I don't think so. I think he was in love with Mistress Bong."

I could see why she had made up a story. Loosened, her rage was carnivorous.

"The man's name?" I said. "The one she came to Boston with."

"I don't know," Daryl said.

"Did you meet him?"

"Yes, but I don't know what his name was. I don't know anything about him. I hated him."

"Can you describe him?"

"No."

I nodded.

"When I was fifteen," Paul said, "my mother was bopping a guy named Stephen, with a ph. He was about six-one, slim, short hair, close-cropped beard, and mustache, always wore aviator glasses with pink lenses."

"So you remember, and I don't," Daryl said.

"I remember them all," Paul said. "Clearly."

"Well, I don't," Daryl said.

Neither of us said anything. Daryl looked out my window. The rain was just getting under way, a few spatters making isolated trickle paths down the pane.

"He was a black man," she said.

I waited.

"Not too big. I think he was only a little taller than my mother. He had a big afro."

"You remember his name?" I said.

She was quiet, watching the evolving rain through my window. Paul and I watched it, too. It was very dark outside.

"My mother called him Leon," she said.

"Last name?" I said.

She shook her head.

"Just Leon," she said. "I assume it was his first name."

I tried to get as much as I could while the faucet was on.

"Any gray in the afro?"

"No."

"Beard?"

"Mustache," she said. "A big Fu Manchu thing."

"You know what he did for a living?"

"No."

"You ever hear from him after she died?"

"No."

"You know where he is now?"

"No."

"You know anything else about him?"

"No."

"He treat you okay?"

"I didn't see much of him. My mother sort of kept him to herself."

"He didn't mistreat you," Paul said.

"No."

The rain arrived like an explosion against the window, flooding the window pane. There was some lightning and commensurate thunder.

I said, "After your mother died, you went to live with your father?"

"Yes."

"How was that?"

She shrugged. "He tried," she said. "But he wasn't much good at anything but rolling a joint. Mostly we were on welfare."

"How'd you get to be an actress?" I said.

"I always wanted to. From as long back as I can remember. I don't know why. I got in the drama club in high school, and the drama club teacher helped me get into an apprentice program at the La Jolla Playhouse and . . ." she spread her hands.

"So why are you so dead set on finding your mother's murderer?" I said.

"Well . . . I . . . she was my mother, for God's sake."

"And you want justice," I said.

"If I can get it," Daryl said.

"I can't promise it," I said.

"I'll settle for revenge," she said.

I looked out the window at the fully evolved thunderstorm. *Blow, winds,* I thought, *and crack your cheeks.*

23

♦ ♦ ♦ ♦ ♦

I called Evan Malone at the number Epstein had given me and got his wife, and made an appointment to come up to his place on Bow Lake to talk with him. On the drive up Route 93, I called Epstein on the cell phone.

"Find anything in D.C. about Shaka?" I said.

"They got a file," Epstein said.

"Can you get it?"

"Classified."

"Don't you have clearance?"

"Need-to-know basis," Epstein said.

"You need to know."

"No," Epstein said. "I'd like to know. But I'm not working on a case which requires me to know it."

"And you can't work on the case because you can't get any information about it to work on it."

"That's a little oversimplified," Epstein said.

"They have no reason to classify some two-bit counterculture gunny from 1974 on a need-to-know," I said.

"Apparently, they do," Epstein said. "I'll try to spring it loose. There are some channels to go through."

"I'll bet there are," I said. "What reason would you guess."

"I don't wish to guess," Epstein said. "I'll see what I can find out."

"I'm guessing there was an informant involved."

"I don't wish to guess," Epstein said.

Malone's cabin, on Bow Lake, was alone in the woods. There were neighbors, I had passed them on the way in, but they weren't in sight from the cabin, and, as I got out of the car in the driveway, I could have been in Patagonia. An aging cocker spaniel came around the corner of the cabin and gave me a token bark before she sat with her tongue out, waiting for me to pat her. After I did, we went around to the front of the house, which faced out toward the lake. Malone and his wife were sitting on the deck, looking at the water. A pitcher of iced tea sat on a little tray table between them. We said hello, and I sat in a canvas-strapped folding deck chair. They didn't offer me any iced tea.

"I'm trying to backtrack an old killing," I said.

"Anne told me," Malone said and

nodded sideways at his wife.

He didn't look good. His eyes were sort of unfocused. His face had sunk under his cheekbones, and he had the sort of thin, flabby look of a man who had lost a lot of weight in a short time. There was a lot of loose skin under his jaw.

"Emily Gordon," I said. "Killed during a holdup at a bank in Audubon Circle."

"Yeah?"

"I believe you were the lead agent on the case."

"Hard to remember," he said.

"But you know it was long enough ago to be hard to remember," I said.

Malone shook his head and didn't say anything. Malone's wife watched him all the time, as if she were afraid he might fall over without warning. She was short and plump with gray-streaked hair that used to be blond, worn in short bangs across her forehead.

"I know there was a Bureau file on the killing," I said. "But I don't seem able to access it."

Malone sipped his iced tea carefully, as if the glass were hard to hold. When he put it back on the tray table, his wife's hand moved to grab the glass if he had trouble. Neither of them said anything. The spaniel had gone to sleep with her head on Mrs. Malone's left foot.

"I wondered if you might have any recollection of what might be in the file."

Malone was slouched in the deck chair, his chin touching his sternum. He wore tan shorts and a yellow polo shirt with blue horizontal stripes, high white tube socks, and brown leather sandals. His legs were pale and thin and blue-veined.

"Mr. Malone has had some very difficult surgery," Mrs. Malone said. "He hasn't gotten his strength back yet."

"I won't be long," I said. "Anything you can tell me?"

"Nothing to tell," Malone said hoarsely. "Wrong place, wrong time. We never found the shooter."

"Did you know his name was Shaka?"

"No."

It was a splendid summer day, 75 degrees with a breeze off the lake.

"Do you know why she was in Boston?"

"Don't remember, something about a sister." There was sweat on Malone's forehead.

"Did you write a report?"

"Must have." He smiled a frightful, weak, humorless smile. "Bureau's big for reports."

"You recall any connection with Sonny Karnofsky?"

"Never heard of him."

No law enforcement guy in Boston in the past thirty years wouldn't have known about Sonny Karnofsky.

"Any kind of mob connection?"

"No." He looked at his wife. She stood at once.

"I'm sorry," she said. "Mr. Malone needs to lie down now."

I nodded. She sort of hovered around him as he got himself slowly out of the chair. He stood as if his balance were uncertain and began to walk very slowly, bent over as if his stomach were vulnerable and he wished to protect it. She was right with him, ready to catch him if he fell. Though how she thought she'd prevent him from falling, I didn't know. They reached the back door of the cabin. She opened it and put her hand under his arm and steered him through. Then she turned and looked at me.

She said, "Good-bye, Mr. Spenser," and went in after him. I looked at the spaniel. She sat up suddenly and scratched her ear with her right hind foot.

"Enjoy," I said to her, and walked back to my car.

24

I drove out the road from Malone's cottage in green shade. The trees pressed close to the small road. I recognized white pine and maple and oak, and some pale-skinned birch. I felt like Natty Bumppo. A half mile from Malone's cottage, a dirt road cut across the paved road. I was twenty yards past it when I spotted a car parked across the pavement. I looked in the rearview mirror. A car pulled out of the dirt road behind me and parked across the pavement. Men got out of both cars and stood behind them. They had long guns. I was pretty sure this wasn't a speed trap. I slowed. There was no way past the car in front of me. I checked the rearview mirror again. There was no way past the car behind me, except that when it had pulled straight out of the dirt road, it had left a little space behind it. I couldn't go straight past it on the pavement, but I might be able to turn onto the dirt road. I didn't have any other choices. I did a really perfect, and really quick, three-point turn and floored it back toward the second car. Behind it, two men raised their guns. Probably shotguns. I slouched down behind the wheel as much as I could, and just before I hit their car I rammed on the brakes and yanked my car as hard right as I could. The car almost stood on its side. But it didn't, and I was onto the dirt road and into the woods. It was barely a road. Something scraped the bottom of my car. I smelled gasoline. The car bucked and stumbled; it went far too fast down through the root-welted, rock-stubbled trace. My right wheel hit an outcropping of granite, and the tire exploded. Ahead of me I could see the glimmer of the lake. I stomped on the brakes and rolled out of the car and hit the ground running. I was wearing jeans and a T-shirt and running shoes. At least I was dressed for it.

To the right was the gray-buckled remnants of a fishing camp. I went past it on the run. I was pretty sure these were city guys behind me. If I got them deep enough into the woods, I might have a chance. I was a city guy, too, but I hadn't always been one.

Behind me I heard the cars pull up, the doors open and close. I had a short-barreled .38 on my hip, but against five or six guys with shotguns, that was pretty much irrelevant. This was a case of *Feet, do your duty.* I slowed to a jog as I moved through the woods. Twisting my ankle on a rock or tripping would be a bad thing. The lake showed itself occasionally, when the forest thinned for a moment. I knew I could run ten miles, and I was hopeful that none of my pursuers could. If they could, carrying shotguns, I was also hopeful that they'd give up before I did. I looked at my watch: 2:30 in the afternoon. The sun would have moved westward enough to get a direction. It was hot in the woods. There were insects. A vast network of thin vines with thorns was everywhere, catching at my pants legs. I was walking now, moving as fast as the forest permitted, keeping the lake on my left. I was glad for the heat and the bugs and the thorny vines. I could put up with it to save my life. I wasn't so sure the shooters could put up with it to kill me. There was an opening in the forest where a big old maple tree had fallen, its upper branches ten feet out into the lake water. I climbed over it and stopped and listened. Distantly, I could hear them thrashing along. I could hear their voices. They were not happy voices. I looked at the lake and the tangle of rotting limbs in the water. Beyond them across an inlet, I could see the imploded fishing hut. We'd been walking around a long inlet for an hour. Straight across, it was about a hundred yards. I could hear my heartbeat, steady but loud and fast from exertion. I took my gun out and went along behind the fallen tree and into the water. Holding the gun high enough to keep it dry, I waded carefully over the underwater rocks, slippery with algae, until I was neck deep among the rotting leaves and branches.

I waited.

They were about ten minutes behind me, five of them, three with shotguns. All but one were wearing street shoes. They were sweat-soaked and angry.

"Shit! . . . I shoulda left the freakin' shotgun in the car. . . . You think he's got a gun? . . . How the fuck do I know? . . . All I know we're supposed to clip him. . . . Yeah, well you blocked the fucking road right we'da had him clipped and gone. . . . Fuck you. . . . Yeah, well fuck you. . . . How the fuck was I supposed to know the asshole would drive into the fucking woods. . . . You're the fucking asshole. . . . Whyn't both of you shut the fuck up. . . ."

They labored past me, sweat-soaked and red-faced. When they had passed, I slipped out from among the branches and headed across the inlet. I could touch the bottom

most of the way. I came out of the lake behind the shack, moving quietly. They could
have left someone with the cars. They
hadn't. The two cars sat silently in the
dappled yard at the end of the dirt road, a
Chrysler LeBaron and a Ford Crown Victoria. I put my gun back in the soaked holster, under the saturated T-shirt, on the
waterlogged belt that held up my wet jeans.
I felt like Burt Reynolds in *Deliverance*. I
looked into both cars. No one had left any
keys. I shrugged as if someone could see
me and opened the hood on the Ford and
pulled the ignition wires free and started
the car by the always reliable hotwire
method. I backed the Ford around and
headed it up the dirt road. Then I got out
and opened up the Chrysler and pulled all
the spark plugs loose from the wires and
threw them into the lake. I got back into
the Ford and drove carefully back up the
dirt road.

25

♦ ♦ ♦ ♦ ♦

Hawk came into my apartment with a long duffel bag. He set it on my coffee table and unzipped it.

"We going to the mattresses?" he said.

"What brings you?" I said.

He took out a 12-gauge pump shotgun and stood it against my kitchen counter. He took out four boxes of shells and put them on my counter.

"Susan."

"I'm surprised she didn't come herself," I said.

"Me too."

"She tell you the whole story?"

"Much as she knows."

"That would be the whole story," I said.

"How come you tell her? Makes her worry."

"If I don't tell her, she'll worry all the time."

" 'Cause she never know if you in danger or not."

"Yes."

Hawk nodded. "How long you think it

took them to walk out of there?" he said.

"Given the woodsmanship they showed me, they might still be in there."

"There more where they came from."

Hawk took an M-16 rifle out of the duffel bag and leaned it next to the shotgun. He took three extra magazines and put them on my counter next to the shotgun shells.

"Sonny?" he said.

"Who else?" I said.

"Harvey with them?"

"No. I guess they figured they wouldn't need him."

"How Sonny know you up there?"

"Could have had a tail on me," I said.

"That you didn't make?"

"Unlikely," I said.

"So?"

"Only people who knew when and where I'd be were the Malones."

Hawk took a Glock semiautomatic handgun out of the bag and put it on the counter along with an extra magazine and three boxes of 9mm shells.

"The cops and the robbers?" Hawk said.

"Wouldn't be a first," I said.

"No," Hawk said. "Wouldn't."

He took a change of clothes out of the bag and folded it on top of the bookcase.

He took out a shaving kit and walked to the bathroom and left it, and came back into the living room and sat on the couch with his feet on the coffee table.

"You got a plan?" he said.

"Be good if we knew why Sonny was interested in this," I said.

"That's not a plan," Hawk said. "A plan be how you going to find out why Sonny interested in this."

"Gimme a minute."

Hawk went around the counter into my kitchen and made himself a peanut-butter sandwich on whole wheat. He found a bottle of champagne in the refrigerator, opened it, and poured some into a pint beer glass and came back around the counter, moved some of his arsenal around to make room for his sandwich, and sat on a stool to have lunch.

"Think of anything yet?" he said.

"How come I always have to think of stuff?" I said.

" 'Cause you the white detective," Hawk said.

"But if I always think of stuff and you don't, it just reinforces the black-white stereotype."

"I know," Hawk said.

"So why don't you think of a plan?" I said.

"You just trying to weasel out 'cause you can't think of no plan," he said.

"Okay, I admit it," I said. "You go."

Hawk grinned. "Brain, do yo' duty," he said.

We were quiet. Hawk looked ruminative. He chewed his sandwich. He sipped his champagne. I stood and walked to my front window and looked down on Marlboro Street. The colleges had closed for the summer, and the summer-school sessions hadn't started. The whole Back Bay seemed empty and pleasant. I could even see a parking space up toward Berkeley Street.

Behind me, Hawk said, "Damn."

"You think of something?" I said.

"No."

I grinned. "You just discovered you're no smarter than I am."

"Startling," Hawk said.

"Maybe we need to work on this together," I said.

"One half-wit plus one half-wit?" Hawk said.

"We can hope," I said.

Hawk poured himself some more champagne. "So how come the mob . . ." Hawk said.

"Or some of it," I said.

"And the FBI . . ."

"Or some of it."

"Both want to cover up the twenty-eight-year-old murder of some hippie broad from San Diego?" Hawk said.

"Nicely restated," I said.

"Thank you — you talk with the husband yet?"

"Daryl's father?"

"Uh-huh."

"San Diego seemed like a long way to go," I said.

"We got no place else to go."

"Excellent point," I said.

26

Susan sat on the bed watching me pack. Pearl loped around my apartment, alert for something to chew.

"What are you going to do about a gun?" Susan said. "It's not a good time to be checking one through."

"Hawk has an arrangement," I said.

"I shudder to think," Susan said.

"If you came, we could stay at La Valencia in La Jolla and eat in their upstairs restaurant with a view of the cove."

"Would there be any sex involved?" Susan said.

"Only with me," I said.

"Oh," Susan said.

We were quiet for a moment. Pearl padded silently into the bedroom and circled my bed and padded silently out. We both watched her.

"I can't leave her yet with someone else," Susan said.

I nodded.

"You understand."

"Better," I said. "I agree."

"But you still wish I could come," Susan said.

I smiled at her.

"Why are you smiling?" she said.

"You are always," I said, "so entirely you."

"Yes," Susan said. "I believe I am."

I finished packing and closed the suitcase.

"How can you exist for several days with what's in that suitcase?" Susan said.

"Astonishing, isn't it?" I sat on the bed beside her. She looked straight at me for a moment, then suddenly she pressed her face against my chest. I put my arms around her. Neither of us said anything. We sat for awhile.

With her voice muffled against my shirt, Susan said, "Hawk will be with you."

"Yes."

"And you are one of the toughest men in creation," she said.

"Also true."

Pearl came back into the bedroom and saw us and came over and sniffed and sat suddenly down and stared at us with her ears cocked slightly forward. After a time, Susan raised her head and kissed me with her mouth open. She pressed herself harder against me.

"Pearl is watching," I said.
"I don't care," Susan said.
Which turned out to be true.

27

At San Diego Airport, a young, athletic-looking black man was waiting for us as we came into the main terminal. He was dressed like a character on television, with a blue-and-white durag under a side-skewed Padres baseball hat. There were a lot of platinum chains, some very expensive basketball shoes, some very baggy jeans, and a Chargers jersey that had SEAU printed across the back. He was carrying a green Adidas gym bag with white stripes on the side and holding a hand-lettered sign that said SPENSER on it.

I said, "I'm Spenser."

He looked at Hawk. Hawk nodded, and the kid gave me the gym bag, folded up his sign, and swaggered away like a guy looking for a fight.

The rental car was a white Volvo sedan. Hawk drove while I opened the bag and, among a couple of towels bunched up for bulk, found two holstered Smith & Wesson nines with four-inch barrels and a stainless satin finish. They each carried ten rounds, plus one in the chamber. There was an extra magazine for each gun and two boxes of Remington 9mm ammunition. I checked one of the guns, and it was loaded, including a round in the chamber. Hawk glanced over as he drove up Route 5.

"Networking," he said.

"Hanging with a thug has its moments," I said.

"I prefers the term 'criminal genius,' " Hawk said.

"Of course you do," I said.

Barry Gordon had a small house in Mission Bay with a narrow view of the water. We pulled up in front, and I got out, with my new gun unholstered and stuck in my hip pocket. Getting the holster on my belt seemed more trouble than I wanted to go through in the car. Hawk waited in the car, listening to a reggae station. The front yard had a low picket fence around it. The fence needed to be painted. Actually, it needed to be scraped, sanded, and painted. The gate hung crooked, its hinges loose. In the small, weedy front lawn, a black Labrador retriever with a red bandana around his neck barked at me without hostility when I pushed the gate open.

Behind me, Hawk lowered the power window and said, "Backup?"

"Fortunately, I'm armed," I said.

Once I was inside, the Lab came over with his tail wagging slowly and his ears flattened, and waited for me to pat him, which I did before I knocked on Barry's door, which needed the same treatment the fence needed. The door opened almost at once.

"Hey," Barry said.

"Hey," I said.

"You Spenser."

"I am."

"So come on in, man."

"Thanks."

Barry was shirtless, wearing only tartan plaid shorts and flip-flop rubber shower sandals. He had a lot of gray hair, which he wore in a single braid that reached the small of his back. His upper body was slim and smooth, with no sign of muscle. The house appeared to have a living room on one side of the stairs and a kitchen on the other. My guess was that there were two bedrooms and a bath upstairs. Barry waved at the living room in general.

"Have a seat, man. Anywhere you'd like."

The choices were limited. He had a daybed covered with a khaki blanket and two cane-backed rocking chairs. A big television sat on a small steamer trunk under the front window, and an old pink princess phone rested on an inverted packing crate. There was a large circular dog cushion in the middle of the room, filled, from the smell, with cedar shavings. The Lab, who had come in when I did, plomped down on it and stretched his legs out to the side and went to sleep. I sat on the daybed.

"You want a glass of water or something?" Barry said.

I shook my head. He sat in one of the rocking chairs. Beside the chair, on what looked to be an orange crate, was a Baggie full of something that looked like oregano but probably wasn't. Beside the Baggie was a package of cigarette papers.

"So," he said. "How's baby Daryl."

"She's quite a good actress," I said. "You ever see her perform?"

"No, man, regrettably, I never got the chance."

"I can see you're a busy guy," I said.

"I write music," he said.

"Of course you do," I said. "What can you tell me about Daryl's mother?"

"Emmy?"

"Emily Gordon," I said.

"Well, shit, man, she died thirty years ago."

"Twenty-eight," I said.

Without looking, Barry extracted a cigarette paper from the packet and picked up his Baggie. "That's a long time ago, man."

He shook out some of the contents of his Baggie and rolled himself a joint. He was expert. He could roll with one hand. He put the joint in his mouth and fumbled with the flat of his hand on the orange crate.

"You got a match?" he said.

"No."

He stood and flip-flopped past the front stairs to the kitchen and came back with a pack of matches. He lit the joint, took a big inhale, and let it out slowly.

"Calmer?" I said.

"Huh? Oh, the joint. I know I smoke too much. I got to cut back one of these days. So what did you want to ask me?"

"Anything you could tell me," I said.

"About Emmy? Well, you know, I haven't seen her in about twenty-eight years."

He took a big drag on the joint and held the smoke in for a time and let it out slowly. He let his head rest against the woven cane back of the rocker. Then he giggled.

"Shit, man, nobody seen her in twenty-eight years, have they?"

"Probably not," I said. "Why did she go to Boston?"

"Always wanted to, I guess. You know how it is, man, you get some vision of a place, you finally got to go look at it, see how it compares."

He took another drag.

"She have a boyfriend?"

Barry shrugged.

"Is that a yes?" I said.

"We had a sort of informal marriage, man. You know?"

"So she had a boyfriend?"

"She had a lot of them."

"But this one she followed to Boston."

"I guess," Barry said.

"You know his name?"

"His name?"

"Barry, are these questions too hard for you?"

"It's been thirty years, man."

"Twenty-eight, and in that time you forgot the name of the guy that your wife ran off with?"

"She didn't run off with him, she followed him, there's a difference."

"Sure there is, what was his name?"

"Coyote," he said. "He was an African-American dude."

"You have any idea where Coyote is now?"

"Naw, man, how would I know that?"

He took a last drag on what was now a very small roach and snipped it and put it on the orange crate.

"What did Coyote do for a living?"

"He was a hippie, man. We all were. Mostly, we ripped off the system. Sold a little dope."

"Welfare?"

"Sure."

"What else do you know about Coyote?"

"What's to know, man? He was part of the movement, you know. We didn't ask a lot of questions. I think he mighta done time."

"Where?"

"Hell, I don't know."

"Maybe California?"

"I guess."

"What was he doing in Boston?"

"Hey, man, you think he calls me up, tells me what he's doing?"

"There were a couple of other women there when Emily was shot," I said. "Any idea who they were?"

"No, man."

"You know any of her friends?"

"Sure. I knew a lot of them."

"What were their names."

"Names? All of them?"

"Yeah."

"Been a long time," he said.

"Give me any you can remember."

"I . . ." he spread his hands. "My head's a little scrambled . . . Bunny."

"Bunny who?"

"Ah Bunny . . . Bunny Lawrence, Lombard. Lombard, Bunny Lombard."

"Excellent, Barry. Gimme another one."

We did this for maybe half an hour, during which time I coaxed three other names from him. I wrote them down. He didn't know where any of them were anymore.

"They were just around, you know, in the movement," he said.

"Okay," I said. "And when Emily was killed, you had sole custody of Daryl."

"Yeah. That's when I got us this house."

"You bought this place after your wife died."

"Yeah. Emmy's parents bought her a little insurance policy when she was born. Typical."

"Typical of what?" I said.

"Middle-class mentality," Barry said. "Have a baby, buy it insurance."

"And you were the beneficiary?"

"No. Emmy changed it to Daryl. But I

was her father, so I used the money to buy her this house."

"Which she still owns?"

"Hey, I been paying the mortgage for twenty-eight years."

"World's best dad," I said. "How long was Daryl with you."

"She took off when she was eighteen."

"You mean she ran away."

"Whatever. We wasn't mad at each other or anything. She just wanted to be on her own."

"You stay in touch?"

"She wrote me sometimes."

I decided not to ask if he wrote her back. Barry started to roll another joint. On his big, cedar-shaving dog cushion, the Lab made some lip-smacking noises in his sleep. He was probably half snookered on secondhand smoke.

"Is there anything else you can think of," I said, "that might help me find who killed your wife."

Barry got his cigarette burning.

"Not a thing, man."

"Ever hear of a guy named Abner Fancy?"

"Abner Fancy, hell no, man. I wouldn't forget a name like Abner Fancy. God-damn."

"Ever hear of a group called the Dread Scott Brigade?"

"Wow," he said, "a blast from the past. The Dread Scott Brigade. Yeah, I think so. I think Emmy had some friends was in Dread Scott. Emmy hung out with a lot of blacks."

"Coyote a member?" I said.

Barry shrugged. He was getting tired.

"Coulda been. I don't know. Mostly I did my music, smoked a little dope." He smiled modestly. "Scored a few ladies myself, you know?"

"Way to go," I said.

I gave him my card. He looked at it.

"Anything occurs to you," I said, "get in touch."

"Hey, man," Barry said. "You're from Boston."

"I am."

"What are you doing out here?"

"I came to talk with you."

"Me? Hey, that's really cool."

"Way cool," I said. "Anything you can think of."

"Sure," Barry said. "Sure thing."

He took in a long pull of marijuana smoke and held it. I walked to the door. Barry was still holding the smoke. As I opened the door, he let it out slowly and smiled pleasantly at me through the smoke.

Reefer madness.

Hawk and I were staying up in La Jolla, at La Valencia. I called Susan. After that, Hawk and I took a run along the cove and had dinner in the hotel restaurant, which was near the top of the hotel and had spectacular views of the Pacific. We each started with a martini.

"It always amazes me," I said to Hawk, "how some kids can grow out of the trash heap they started in."

"Daryl?" Hawk said.

I nodded.

"Her mother," I said, "apparently slept with everybody that would hold still long enough and then got murdered. Her father did dope until he turned into a mushroom. And she grows out of that, apparently on her own, to become a functioning adult and a good actress."

The sun was almost touching the far rim of the ocean. Five pelicans swung over the cove, flying in an orderly arrangement. The last two divers came out of the water. I drank a little of my martini. Hawk's martini was the traditional straight up with olives. Always the rebel, I had mine on the rocks with a twist. I sipped again. The martini tasted like John Coltrane sounds.

"A little like Paul," Hawk said.

"Yeah," I said. "But Paul had me. Who has she had?"

Hawk looked out at the wide, slow ocean, with the evening beginning to settle onto it.

"Maybe she have a lot of stuff in her," Hawk said.

"Maybe."

"And maybe she have Paul," Hawk said.

I thought about it, and so as not to waste time while I was thinking, I drank some more martini.

"I don't know if he's known her long enough," I said.

"Paul a smart kid," Hawk said.

"I know."

"And he pretty strong," Hawk said.

"He is."

"Got from his uncle," Hawk said.

"Uncle Hawk?"

"Sho' nuff."

"Jesus Christ," I said.

29
♦ ♦ ♦ ♦ ♦

In the morning, Hawk and I ate huevos rancheros outside on the patio. Then we strapped on our rental guns, got in our rental car, and headed for the 405.

It's a two-and-a-half-hour drive from San Diego to L.A., unless Hawk drives, in which case it's just less than two hours. At twenty past noon we checked into the Beverly Wilshire Hotel at the foot of Rodeo Drive.

"This pretty regal," Hawk said in the high marble lobby, "for a couple of East-Coast thugs with loaner guns."

"We deserve no less," I said.

"We deserve a lot less," Hawk said. "But I won't insist on it."

Captain Samuelson had his office in the Parker Center. I left Hawk outside on Los Angeles Street with the car. It saved parking, and I figured Sonny Karnofsky wouldn't make a run at me inside LAPD Headquarters.

Samuelson's office was on the third floor in the Robbery Homicide Division, in a section marked Homicide Special Section I. Samuelson came out of his office in his shirt sleeves. He was fully bald now, his head clean shaven, and he'd gotten rid of his mustache. But he still wore tinted aviator glasses, and he was still one of my great fans.

"The hot dog from Boston," he said, standing in his office doorway.

"I thought I'd swing by," I said. "Help you straighten out the Rampart Division."

"Not possible," Samuelson said. "Besides, I'm out of town, fishing in Baja, won't be back until you've left town."

"You can run," I said, "but you can't hide."

Samuelson jerked his head and stood aside, and I went into his office. I walked in and sat and looked around.

"Slick," I said.

"I'm a fucking Captain," Samuelson said. "Section commander. Of course I have a slick office. Whaddya want?"

"Coyote, don't know his real name," I said. "Formerly of San Diego. Black, about sixty. Maybe done time. Maybe for possession with intent."

"You think I know every two-bit dope slug in the city?" Samuelson said.

"Yes."

142

Samuelson took out a package of Juicy Fruit gum, unwrapped two sticks, and folded them into his mouth. He held the package out toward me. I shook my head.

"Every time I chew gum," I said, "I bite the inside of my cheek."

"Clumsy bastard," Samuelson said.

"Have trouble walking, too," I said.

Samuelson nodded and swung his swivel chair around to a computer on a table at a right angle to his desk.

"See what I can pull up," he said.

He played with the computer for a couple minutes. "Okay," he said, reading off the screen. "Holton, Leon James, AKA Coyote. Born in Culver City, February tenth, 1940. First arrest in San Diego, August eleventh, 1953, for assault, dismissed because the plaintiff never showed. October 1960, in San Diego, suspicion of armed robbery, lack of evidence. List goes on. I'll print it out for you."

Samuelson tapped the keyboard.

"He did time in 1966 for armed robbery," Samuelson said, still reading. "And in 1980 for dope."

"Long dry spell," I said.

"Both those collars were in San Diego, too," Samuelson said.

"Anything else interesting?"

"You first," Samuelson said.

Seemed fair. I told him what I knew about Emily and Daryl and Barry and Leon.

"Ah, yes," Samuelson said and leaned back in his chair. "Flower power. That sounds like our Leon, doesn't it?"

"Lot of drugs around," I said.

"Liberated," Samuelson said. "Lot of pussy, too."

"Now you tell me," I said.

Samuelson was looking at the screen as we talked.

"This is kind of interesting," he said. "Had a couple of FBI inquiries on Leon. Late '74, early '75. Local SAC requested any information we had."

"What did you give him?"

"I'm using the term 'we' loosely. I wasn't even around here then."

"Sorry, I just assume you know everything. How about any of these names?"

"Yeah, sure. Why don't you try your pal del Rio. He knows a lot about crime in Southern California."

"Being the source of much of it," I said. "He's in Switzerland with his, ah, staff."

"For crissake," Samuelson said. "You called him first."

"I didn't want to bother you," I said.

"Then stay the fuck back in Boston and eat beans," Samuelson said. "You bother me every time you get west of Flagstaff."

"Well, I guess I should go see Leon," I said. "Got an address?"

"No. But he's on parole," Samuelson said. "His PO is Raymond Cortez."

"You got a phone number?"

"Sure."

"So why don't you call Raymond and ask for Leon's address."

"What am I, your secretary?"

"L.A. Police Captain will get a lot more response than a private guy from Boston," I said.

"And should," Samuelson said and picked up his phone.

Leon had an address on Mulholland Drive, west of Beverly Glen. Samuelson wrote it out on a memo pad, ripped off the sheet, and handed it to me.

"Thank you," I said. "How about a woman named Bunny Lombard?"

"Bunny?" Samuelson said.

"Only name I got," I said.

Samuelson leaned forward and tapped his computer keys.

"I feel like I'm on a fucking quiz show," he said.

"You are an absolute model of transcontinental cooperation," I said.

Samuelson studied the computer a little longer, then he shook his head.

"Nix on Bunny," he said. "Nothing."

"I got plenty of that," I said.

"And deserve every bit of it," Samuelson said.

"I may as well go see Leon."

"You got any backup? This is a tough coast. Leon may be a tough guy."

I nodded. "I have backup," I said.

"He any good?" Samuelson said.

"Captain," I said. "You have no idea."

30

♦ ♦ ♦ ♦ ♦

It was one of those days in L.A. There was enough breeze to keep the smog diluted, and the sun was bright and pleasant, shining down on the flowering trees and blond hair. At quarter till two we were heading up Beverly Glen. At the top we turned left onto Mulholland and went along the crest of the hill with the San Fernando Valley spread out below us to the right, orderly and smog-free.

Leon Holton's house was built onto a hillside at the end of a long driveway that slanted off Mulholland so that the house overlooked the Valley. When we pulled up to the security gate and rang the bell, a voice on the speakerphone said, "Yeah?"

"We're here to see Leon Holton," I said. "Emily Gordon sent us."

There was a long silence, then the intercom buzzed and the security barrier swung open. We drove another hundred yards and parked in a circular driveway outside. The house in front of us was some sort of glass pyramid with a wide double door recessed into the front. The door was painted turquoise. To the left, built into the down slope toward the valley, was a full-sized basketball court made of some kind of green composition from which tennis courts are sometimes built. A red, white, and blue basketball sat on the ground near midcourt. A slim black man with a small patch of beard under his lower lip came to the door as we got out of the car.

"I'd like to see some ID, please," he said.

"We're not cops," I said.

The slim guy was wearing a black Armani suit and a black silk T-shirt. He glanced quickly over his shoulder into the house. Then he turned back and stared at us for a time.

"Getting a little scared?" I said to Hawk.

"Chilled," Hawk said. "The man's stare is chilling."

"Who's this Emily Gordon?" the slim man said.

"You Leon?" I said.

"No. What's this shit about Emily whosis?"

"We'll need to talk with Leon about that," I said.

The slim guy looked at us some more. Hawk and I bore up as best we could. Finally, the slim guy said, "Wait here," and turned and disappeared into the ridiculous glass pyramid. We waited. In a few minutes he came back out, and with him was backup. There was a little white guy with big hands who looked like he might have been a jockey once, and a 300-pound black man with very little body fat who stood about 6'8".

"If there's trouble," I murmured to Hawk, "you take him."

"Might be better," Hawk said, "we run like rabbits."

"We need to search you," the slim guy said, "before you go in."

"We each have a gun," I said.

"Can't bring in no gun," the slim man said.

"We'll lock them in the trunk," I said.

"I'll do it," Slim said. "Pop the trunk."

I did.

"Now, first, White Guy, take the gun out and hold it in two fingers and hand it to me."

I did and he took it, and, holding it in his left hand, he went around to Hawk.

"Now you, bro."

Hawk gave him his gun. Slim put both guns in the trunk.

"Okay," he said. "Step out, put your hands on the roof."

We did. The big black man stood close

to us. The jockey stood away a little and at an angle. The big guy was muscle. The jockey would be the gun hand. Slim patted us down and stepped away.

"Okay," he said.

The whole first floor of the pyramid was without walls. Seen from the inside the glass had a bluish tint, as if we were standing inside an aquarium. In the center of the space was an open fire pit with a stainless steel hood and stainless steel chimney. There was a big fire in the fireplace and a lot of air-conditioning to overcome it. In the far left-hand corner was a small glass elevator with stainless steel trim. The vast space was furnished as a living room, with stainless steel and blue leather furniture, and several big television screens suspended in midair. It was bigger than O'Hare Airport, but not as warm. There was a black man sitting beyond the fireplace in a stainless steel and blue leather Barcalounger. Slim pointed us out to him. Then he and his helpers went and stood near the front door.

Leon didn't get up when we walked over. He was a taut, middle-sized black man with noticeable cheekbones, wearing rimless glasses. His graying hair was cut in a short afro, and he wore a long, blue-patterned dashiki. His feet were bare. There was a prison gang tattoo on his left forearm. He and Hawk looked at each other for a long time.

"Who is Emily Gordon?" Leon said softly.

His voice was flat and controlled and careful, as if he thought about every word.

"You were with her in Boston," I said. "In 1974."

"Never heard of her."

"You let us in here," I said, "so you could find out what we knew about her . . . and you."

Leon's gaze was steady. He made no comment. Hawk appeared to be paying no attention to either of us or anything else. But I knew that he was taking in the room. If the balloon went up, he'd know where he was.

"I'll make it easy," I said. "We know that you and she were an item. We know you went to Boston and she went with you, or after you, it's not clear which. And she was in a bank during a holdup and got shot."

Leon neither spoke nor moved. There was about him a sense of contained energy that could explode if jostled. I jostled it some more.

"What do you know about the Dread Scott Brigade?"

"Nothing."

"Know a guy named Abner Fancy?" I said. "Called himself Shaka?"

"No."

"Bunny Lombard?"

"No."

"How about a really bad asshole named Coyote?"

"Nothing about him," Leon said.

I glanced around the vast, inhospitable room.

"This the house that dope built?" I said.

"I came into some money," Leon said.

"A lot."

"Yes," he said. "A lot."

"You have any idea who shot Emily Gordon?" I said.

"Don't know," he said. "Don't care."

I took out my card and handed it to him.

"You think of anything," I said, "give me a shout."

He took the card and looked at it and tore it in half and dropped it on the floor.

"Or not," I said.

Leon gestured at Slim. "You and Tom can go now," he said.

Hawk looked at him for a moment. "When you in the joint, Coyote," Hawk

152

said. "How many guys you punk for?"

Leon's face got tighter, but he didn't speak. Slim and his associates led us back to the car, where, as soon as I got there, I opened the trunk and took out the two guns and gave one to Hawk. I saw the slim guy tense a little. The jockey licked his lips. Hawk and I got in the car and drove away.

31

We were driving back down the hill on Beverly Glen.

"Leon ain't pushing loose joints in pool rooms," Hawk said.

"Unless he pushed an awful lot of them," I said. "What do you think?"

"We didn't learn much," Hawk said. " 'Cept that he knew Emily Gordon. He pretty much admitted that the minute he let us in."

"Had to ask," I said.

" 'Course you did," Hawk said. "Can't know what's going to happen before you go in."

"We accomplished something, though," I said.

"Got to see inside the mansion," Hawk said.

"Well, yeah, that's worth something. We also got another reason to look behind us when we walk."

Hawk grinned. "Keep us alert," he said.

We wound down past the Glen Market, where I had once bought a bottle of champagne to drink with Candy Sloan.

"If I weren't a master detective," I said, "I'd be getting frustrated."

"You been walking around all these years thinking you a master detective?" Hawk said.

At the foot of the hill, I followed the tricky little zigzag across Sunset.

"I have been detecting the ass off of this thing now for what, two weeks? I know that Daryl's childhood is made up. I know her mother was in Boston on promiscuous business. I know her father's a dope fiend. I know that the people who did the robbery are headed by a black guy named Abner Fancy, who calls himself Shaka. I know that Emily's promiscuous business in Boston was probably with Leon Dope King, who's a black guy. I know somebody in the FBI wants this thing covered up. I know that Sonny Karnofsky wants it covered up. I know there's a connection between Malone, the retired FBI guy, and Karnofsky."

" 'Cause Sonny try to hit you coming from his house and nobody else know you be there."

"Wow," I said. "You must be a master detective, too."

Hawk nodded, looking at the expensive

155

houses of uncertain lineage that lined the flat of Beverly Glen.

"And you put all that together. . . ." Hawk said.

"And you got squat," I said.

"And several people trying to kill you."

"Being a master detective has its downside," I said.

"Wonder if Leon is Shaka," Hawk said.

"Your guy told me Abner Fancy was Shaka."

"Maybe Abner and Leon the same guy."

At Wilshire, I turned right.

"We not going to the hotel."

"Driving helps me think," I said.

"Something better," Hawk said.

We were heading west along the Wilshire corridor, where the high-rise condos lined Wilshire Boulevard like palisades.

"Why Boston?" I said.

"Why not," Hawk said.

"It's a question we haven't asked, because we started out thinking that Emily came to visit her sister."

"We haven't asked?" Hawk said.

"But she didn't," I said. "She came chasing Leon. So what was Leon doing in Boston."

"Being as how I a bad guy," Hawk said. "I know 'bout bad guys, and most of us, if we in California, don't sit 'round saying, 'Hey, man, le's go over to Boston and hoist us a bank.' "

"So, maybe someone was from Boston."

"Maybe," Hawk said. "How we going to find out who?"

"I'll detect some more," I said.

" 'Less somebody shoot your ass," Hawk said.

" 'Less that," I said.

32

Hawk put our guns in a locker at the airport, put the key in an envelope, and dropped the envelope in the mail. We got on American Flight 12, and five-and-a-half hours later Vinnie picked us up at Logan and handed each of us our very own gun.

"Did they behave while we were gone?" I said.

"Who?" Vinnie said.

"The firearms."

"The guns?"

"Yeah."

"Are you fucking crazy?" Vinnie said.

"Man's without sentiment," Hawk said.

"You're as fucking goofy as he is," Vinnie said.

Vinnie drove us home through the new Ted Williams Tunnel, which was not yet open to the general public. I raised this point with Vinnie.

"I am not the freakin' general public," Vinnie said.

We went through the tunnel without incident.

In the morning I called Daryl, and at 10 a.m., with Hawk lounging on the couch, I sat in my office and drank coffee and talked with her.

"I'm half awake," she said. "We had a performance last night."

"Coffee is the answer," I said.

She smiled. "To everything?"

"No. Sometimes there needs to be orange juice too."

"Did you see my father?" she said.

"I did."

"Isn't he a jerk?"

I nodded. "He is," I said.

She shook her head sadly. "He couldn't control himself," she said. "Let alone control my mother."

"Leon's last name was Holton. That ring any bells?"

"No."

"How about Abner Fancy?"

"What kind of name is that?"

"A funny one," I said. "You ever hear it?"

"No."

"Do you remember any of your mother's friends?" I said. "Anywhere?"

"In her whole life?"

"Yes. Any names come to mind? Even if you've only heard of them?"

"My mom died when I was six, for God's sake."

"I'm almost as keenly aware of that as you are. Any names?"

"Bunny," she said. "One of the people my mom was with in Boston was named Bunny. I remember because I always thought of a huge white rabbit hopping along."

"Bunny Lombard?"

"Could be," Daryl said. "I don't think I ever heard a last name."

"How did your mother know her?"

"I think they were in college together," Daryl said.

"Your mother went to college?"

"A year or two, then she dropped out."

"Where?"

"Some school around here," Daryl said.

"Here?"

"Boston. Starts with a T."

"Tufts?"

"No."

"Taft?"

"Yes, that's it. Taft University."

I looked at Hawk, draped on my couch. He looked back at me and smiled widely.

"It would have been good to know that sooner."

"Why? What difference would it have made?"

"If you want me to find who killed your mother," I said, "then you give me whatever you know, and let me decide if it will make a difference."

"Well, you don't have to get all rumpled up about it."

"The hell I don't," I said. "What else haven't you told me? Do you know how she met Leon?"

"No."

"Did your aunt go to Taft?"

"She's older than my mother. I think she went first."

"She stay in school?"

"I don't know."

"Why did Leon and your mother come to Boston?"

"I don't know."

"How'd you get here?"

"We drove. Leon and Mom and me."

"Besides Bunny," I said, "did you meet anyone here?"

"We stayed with my aunt; there were people coming and going."

"What can you tell me about them?" I said.

She stared at me with her lips tight and began to cry.

I looked at Hawk. He had his head back, examining the ceiling.

"I know it's hard," I said. "But I don't know how else to get information."

"Why are you so awful?" she said.

"Must be a gift," I said.

She stood suddenly and left the room without another word. Hawk continued his examination of the ceiling.

"Sure do know how to question a client," he said.

I nodded slowly, looking at the open door through which my client had departed.

"Master detective," I said.

33

We drove up Cambridge Street to Government Center. Hawk said he would stay with the car while I talked with Epstein.

"You both have an interest in crime," I said.

"Our perspectives differ," Hawk said.

Epstein stood when I came into his office, but he didn't come around the desk to shake hands. Warm, but not effusive.

"Your retired agent is connected to a mobster named Sonny Karnofsky."

"Malone?"

"Yep. You familiar with Sonny?"

"I know the name," Epstein said. "You got a story?"

I told him about the ambush up at Bow Lake. While he listened, he put his elbows on the desk with his hands tented and the index fingers resting against his chin. When I finished, he sat silently, tapping the tips of his fingers together softly. I waited. After a time, he took in a deep breath.

"This sucks," he said.

"Think how I feel."

"Can you identify any of the people who tried to shoot you?"

"No."

"You saw them."

"At a distance," I said. "And briefly."

"Not even a possible?" Epstein said.

"Sorry," I said. "I was distracted by my attempts to flee."

Epstein nodded. I saw no sign of sympathy. "So what, exactly, am I supposed to do about this?" he said.

"If I knew what you were supposed to do," I said, "I might know what I was supposed to do. In the meantime maybe we can take solace in one another."

"Misery loves company," Epstein said.

"Madly," I said.

Epstein leaned back in his chair and put his feet up on his desk. He seemed to be admiring the gloss on his black wingtips.

"What's frustrating is that we know so much and can prove so little," Epstein said.

"We could propound a theory," I said.

Epstein, his feet still up on his desk, put his hands behind his head and recrossed his ankles.

"Go ahead," he said. "Pro-fucking-pound."

"Okay," I said. "I know there's some-

164

thing wrong with this case, Quirk knows it, and you know it. And we all three know that someplace up the family tree, the Bureau wants this case covered up."

Epstein nodded.

"And so does Sonny Karnofsky," I said.

Nod.

"And the link between them is Malone."

"And the loose cannon rolling around in it all is you," Epstein said.

"Humble but proud," I said.

"You got someone watching your back," Epstein said.

"I do."

"Good," Epstein said. "Your theory say what the connection is?"

"Not yet," I said. "That's why I stopped by."

"I got no theory," Epstein said.

"No, but you could find out if there had been some connection between Karnofsky and Malone when Malone was working for the Bureau. Or if Malone was involved in the Emily Gordon thing. Or both."

"I could do that," Epstein said.

"And maybe you could find out what there is to find out about Karnofsky's family."

"I could do some of that, too. And I'm doing this because?"

165

"Because you care about the Bureau," I said. "And this whole thing is frying your ass."

Epstein was silent for awhile, as if he were thinking about things.

"You were a cop once," he said after awhile.

I nodded.

"You remember why?"

"Yep."

"And you quit."

"Yes I did."

"You remember why?"

"Yep."

"I'm an organization man," Epstein said. "I don't want to quit."

"So you can look into Malone and Karnofsky, and Karnofsky's family?"

"You think he's got a family member involved."

"He made a passing allusion," I said. "And while you're at it, you might want to see if you got anything in the system on Leon Holton or Abner Fancy. I know Holton did time in the California prison system. And I'll bet Fancy has done time someplace. Fancy may be AKA Shaka."

"Shaka?"

"Shaka."

"Like in Shaka Zulu."

166

"Just like that."

"Where do these guys come in?"

I told him.

"I'll see what I can do," he said. "I cannot spend Bureau money entirely at my own discretion."

"Me either," I said.

"At least you're getting a fee."

"Yeah."

"How much you make on something like this?"

"Thinking of going private?" I said.

"Just curious."

"For this particular gig," I said, "I've received six Krispy Kreme donuts."

Epstein looked at me silently for a time. Then he smiled. "Lucky bastard," he said.

34

Hawk was driving a silver Lexus that year. It had one of those E-ZPass things mounted on the windshield, and we zipped through the Allston tolls on the Mass. Pike without hesitation.

"Did you acquire that transponder legally?" I said.

"No," Hawk said.

"At least you're consistent," I said.

"Guy behind us oughta have one, too," Hawk said.

"Somebody's behind us?"

"Blue Chevy," Hawk said. "Was behind us on Storrow, too. Then he got hung up in the exact-change lane, and now he's busting his ass to catch us."

I turned in my seat and looked out the back window.

"Third car behind us?" I said.

"Uh-huh."

"Picked us up on Storrow?"

"Be my guess he picked us up front of your place," Hawk said. "And I didn't make him until Storrow."

"You see who it is?"

"Nope. Maybe all day, all Sonny?" Hawk said.

"Could be," I said. "On the other hand, there's folks in the FBI might want to know what I'm up to. If they picked us up in front of my place, then they know there's two of us."

"They do," Hawk said. "But they might not know one of us is me."

"So they might be overconfident?" I said.

"Might," Hawk said. "What you want me to do with them?"

"We'll go about our business," I said. "If they're Feds, they're welcome to tag along. If they're from Sonny and they try to kill us, we'll try to prevent them."

"Wha's this we, Whitey? They ain't after me."

"You have to protect me," I said. "I'm your only friend."

The Chevy tailed inconspicuously along behind us. Sometimes, on stretches without exits, it would pull past us and drive along two or three cars ahead. As we approached exits, it dropped back. It was several cars back when we took the Walford exit.

Taft University was on a series of low

169

hills along both sides of Walford Road, about a half mile from the Pike. The main entrance road curved up the tallest of the hills, past some dormitories, toward the administration building, which formed one side of a big quadrangle at the top. Hawk parked next to a sign that read FACULTY PARKING ONLY. The Chevy pulled in on the other side of the road, back down the hill a little in front of a dormitory. A mixed field of summer-school students was playing touch football on the lawn.

"Let's just sit for a minute," I said.

Hawk nodded, and we sat.

The Chevy sat.

We sat.

Nobody got out of the Chevy.

"As you so sensitively pointed out," I said, "if they are interested in bodily harm, they're after me, not you."

"Uh-huh."

"So if I got out and you drove off, they'd come after me, and we'd know. Or they wouldn't, and we'd know."

"Uh-huh."

"And if they're from Sonny and bear me ill will, and if you hadn't driven very far off, you could appear and descend upon them like the wolf upon the fold."

"Or," Hawk said, "I see there only be

three or four of them and figure I like your odds, and I drive back to Boston."

"I prefer the wolf upon the fold," I said.

Hawk shrugged. "Okay," he said.

"If there will be shooting, we need to do this where a couple dozen college kids won't get cut down in the first volley."

"Don't make no difference to me," Hawk said.

"I know that."

We sat some more. The Chevy sat some more. The touch football game flourished on the lawn. I'd spent some time at Taft with a power forward named Dwayne Woodcock, and again looking into the murder of a girl named Melissa Henderson. I thought about how the campus was laid out.

"Okay," I said. "I'll get out here and walk down that hill past the pond toward the field house. You pull away up past the library and into the quadrangle. Park on the other end, closest to the field house, and see what's up. If they come after me, you come lippity-lop to my rescue."

"Lippity-lop?"

"Yeah. Like Br'er Rabbit. I'm trying to bridge the racial gap."

"Let it gap," Hawk said.

"You got anything but the handgun?" I said.

"Usual selection in the trunk. You carrying that little .38?"

"No need to be offensive," I said. "It's got a two-inch barrel."

"Yeah. You Irish. You think that's long."

"Long enough," I said.

"Sho," Hawk said. "Can't miss from three feet."

I got out of the car and closed the door behind me, and Hawk drove off. There was a long, grassy slope ahead of me with a pond to the left, where some kids lay on blankets, drinking beer. A portable radio was playing music I didn't recognize. On one blanket, the kids were necking. College is great, except for the classes. Behind me, I heard a car start. I kept walking, not in a hurry, but as if I had a destination. I heard tires crunch on the roadside gravel behind me. Hawk, of course, was right about my gun. I was wearing a short-nosed Smith & Wesson .38, butt forward on my left side. It was a comfortable gun to wear and effective at close range. But from where I was to where they were, I'd be lucky to hit the car. Left of the pond, back up the slope, was the library end of the quadrangle. I was careful not to look for Hawk.

Past the pond and to my right stood the field house where Dwayne Woodcock had shaved some points and Clint Stapelton had practiced his big serve. It seemed quite still on the warm June day. Behind me, a car door slammed, and then another and a third. *One front seat, two backseat,* I thought. We had some distance on the college kids now. I slowed down a little. I could hear my breath going in and out. I could smell the pond smell now. The muscles across my shoulders were tightening, and I couldn't make them stop. I bore right, skirting the pond, strolling on the campus, unaware and free of care. I was aware of my heartbeat. Near the edge of the pond, I stopped for a moment and crouched down to tie my shoe. While I was down there, I took out the .38 and cocked it and palmed it. I have big hands. When I straightened up, the gun was barely visible. I was at the far end of the pond, almost to the field house, when they caught up with me. I could hear their footsteps. Then the footsteps stopped, and I heard a thud and a grunt and simultaneously from up the hill the sound of a rifle. I dropped to my knees and spun in the same motion with the .38 out in front of me. There were two standing uncertainly, and between them on the ground, a fat guy in dark pants was sprawled facedown with his arms stretched out as if he had started to dive. A foot from his open right hand lay a 9mm Glock with a silencer screwed into its nose.

"Freeze right there," I said.

Both men had guns out, but they were in a crossfire and hesitated. Then one of them raised his gun and I shot him. The third man threw his gun away and sank to his knees with his hands in the air.

"Don't," he said. "Don't."

The car that had parked at the roadside spun gravel as it pulled away.

"Facedown," I said. "Lace your fingers behind your head."

"Absolutely," he said, as he flopped facedown. "Absolutely."

I looked up the hill. The blue Chevy was gone. I glanced toward the back of the library. Hawk's car was gone. I bent and patted down the guy who was still alive. He was clean. I put my gun away. Then I picked up his gun and the silenced Glock and the Colt 9 that the third guy had been carrying, and, one by one, threw them into the middle of the pond. At the top of the hill, Hawk's car appeared. I went to the prone guy and put my foot in the middle of his back.

"Tell Sonny that he's starting to annoy me," I said.

Then I turned and went uphill to the car. I ran up to show that I could, and maybe somebody had called the cops. Hawk must have thought the same, because he roared away while I was still closing my door, and in ten seconds we were doing 50. I buckled my seat belt.

"What'd you use?" I said.

"Model 70," he said.

"Winchester," I said, "five-round magazine, bolt action?"

"And a scope," Hawk said.

"Oh, hell, a scope. That's no fair."

"No," Hawk said. "It ain't."

35

According to the papers the next morning, two men had been shot at Taft University and two getaway cars were being sought. Two other men were said to have escaped on foot as police searched the campus and surrounding woods. Both were described as white males, as were the victims.

"For crissake," I said to Hawk. "Nobody even saw you."

"I run off lippity-lop," Hawk said.

"You ready to make another try at Taft," I said, "in your car?"

"Be a number of policemen still around," Hawk said.

"Got nothing to do with us," I said. "I'm working on a case. You're my trusty sidekick."

"Long as I don't have to call you Kemo Sabe."

"Ever wonder what that meant?" I said.

"I always thought it meant Paleface Motherfucker," Hawk said.

"That's probably it," I said.

No one followed us this time when we

drove out to Taft. There was some crime scene tape down by the pond and several state police cars parked near the administration building. Hawk stayed in the car. I got out. Nobody paid much attention to either one of us.

Inside the registrar's office, I had to ratchet up my virile charm a little to get past the grim woman at the counter. But I did, and she took my card in and came back and said I could go into the inner office.

"I'm Betty Holmes," she said. "Are you involved in the investigation?"

"Yes," I said.

"Do you have any idea who shot those men?"

"We have some possibilities," I said.

She was maybe fifty, a tall, pale blonde woman with a strong nose, her hair pulled back tightly, and a gleam of intelligence in her eyes. She looked at me silently for a moment. I could see her thinking.

"Who's we?" she said.

"Me," I said. "I was trying to deceive you."

"How charming," she said. "What is it you are actually doing?"

"I'm investigating the death of a woman who went here probably in the late 1960s."

"Which has nothing to do with the recent shootings," she said.

"I don't know what has to do with what," I said. "But I'm not here to investigate the shooting."

"Well," she said, "good. At least now we know what we're talking about."

"Sort of," I said. "Could you see if you have any record of Emily Gold? Or a woman named Lombard."

"If they attended, we would have a record. What is Ms. Lombard's first name?"

"I don't know. She's been referred to as Bunny Lombard, but I assume it's a nickname."

"One would assume," she said. "But, working here, I've encountered some unusual names."

She wrote the names on a piece of paper.

"While you're at it," I said, "see if you have any record of Leon Holton or Abner Fancy."

"What was the second one?"

"Fancy," I said. "Abner Fancy."

She smiled but didn't comment. "Why do you want these names?" she said.

"Emily Gold is the victim. Others are names associated with her at the time of her death."

"She would be," Betty Holmes did some brief addition in her head, "in her fifties."

"She was murdered, probably in her late

twenties," I said. "In 1974."

"And you're still working on the case?"

"On behalf of her daughter," I said.

She thought about it for a little while. I sat and waited quietly, shimmering with virile charm. It worked again, as she summoned the grim woman from out front and dispatched her to find the names.

"Have you always been a private detective," Betty Holmes said.

"I was once a cop," I said.

"And?"

"And I've always been inner-directed," I said.

"But you still wanted to be a detective."

"I'm good at this," I said.

"And one can make a living?"

"I can," I said.

The grim guardian returned with some computer printouts. She looked at me with disapproval. I did not stick out my tongue at her. Betty Holmes looked at the printouts for awhile.

"Emily Gold enrolled with the class of 1967 in September of 1963. She left school in June of 1965 at the end of her sophomore year. We have a Bonnie Lombard in the same class. She left school in January of 1965. We have no Leon Holton or, sadly, an Abner Fancy."

"Addresses?"

"Yes. Nearly thirty years old," she said.

"Got to start somewhere."

"Here," she said.

I took the printout. Emily had an address on Torrey Pines Road in La Jolla. In her final semester she'd gotten four D's and a C. Bonnie Lombard had an address in Paradise.

"How do I get the names of some classmates?" I said.

"Why?"

"I'm floundering," I said. "I have lots of information and no proof. Rule Seven of the inner-directed sleuth operating manual says, when you don't have enough proof, learn anything you can."

"Rule Seven," she said.

"Yes, Ma'am."

She smiled. "Our alumni secretary should be able to help you with that," she said.

"Could you direct me to him?" I said. "And maybe make a phone call to get me by the Gorgon at the gate."

"Gorgon at the gate," she said and laughed and reached for her phone. "Do all detectives talk that way?"

"Most of them are less inner-directed," I said.

There were 3,180 kids in the class that started at Taft in September of 1963. Hawk lay on the couch in my office with his ankles crossed and a Homestead Grays cap tilted down over his eyes, while I went through the list. Emily Gold was there among the G's. Bonnie Lombard was there among the L's. I recognized no other names.

"If we divided this list equally between us," I said to Hawk, "we'd each have only fifteen-something-hundred people to interview."

"One thousand five hundred ninety," Hawk said. "And who gonna keep them from shooting your ass while I'm off chatting with my half?"

"Oh, yeah," I said. "I forgot about that."

"You want to be the one tells Susan I let them kill you?"

"There's something wrong with that question," I said. "But no, I don't."

"So maybe you need to winnow the list," Hawk said.

"Winnow?" I said.

"Glean."

"Absolutely," I said. "I could winnow geographically, and glean all the names in the Boston area."

"You know," Hawk said, "we checked out Bonnie Lombard we might not have to winnow and glean no more."

"Why didn't I think of that," I said.

"You white," Hawk said.

"I do the best I can," I said.

It was hot enough for air-conditioning as we drove along the North Shore toward Paradise and turned off into the old part of town. Paradise was a fishing town gone upscale. There were still fishing boats in the harbor, but the pleasure boats now outnumbered them, and Paradise Neck, across the causeway, was some of the most expensive real estate in Massachusetts.

"Don't appear that Bonnie Lombard be going hungry," Hawk said, as we drove across the causeway with the harbor on our left and the gray Atlantic ocean rolling in to our right.

"Probably had her own room, too," I said.

"How many brothers you think I going to see out here?"

"Well," I said. "These people might have servants."

Seventeen Ocean Street was a rolling lawn behind a fieldstone fence topped by a big gray-shingled Victorian house with a slate roof. There was no gatehouse, but a black Chrysler was parked at the foot of the driveway, its nose toward the street, effectively blocking the way. When we pulled up, a hard-looking guy in a black suit got out and walked over to us.

"That be the chauffeur?" Hawk said.

"You bet," I said and rolled down my window.

"How you doing?" I said.

"Can I help you?" the chauffeur said.

It wasn't unfriendly. It wasn't warm. It was flat and neutral and told me nothing.

"I'm a detective," I said. "I'm trying to locate a woman named Bonnie Lombard."

"Nobody here by that name," the chauffeur said.

"Who lives here now?" I said.

"None of your business," the chauffeur said.

Again, neither threatening nor friendly, simply a statement.

"Okay," I said. "How long have they lived here."

The chauffeur didn't even bother to answer that. He simply shook his head.

"Well," I said. "Nice talking with you."

As we drove away, Hawk said, "Maybe he wasn't the chauffeur."

"What the hell was that all about?" I said.

"There another guy in the car," Hawk said.

"I know."

"Seem kind of unfriendly for a nice suburban family," Hawk said. "Even a rich white one."

"Makes one curious."

"It do."

We drove back across the causeway and found the town library and went in. In the reference section, we found the town directory, which listed residents by address, and found that the property at 17 Ocean Street was owned by Sarno Karnofsky.

"Would that be the elegant and charming Sonny?" I said.

"I believe it would," Hawk said.

Curiouser and curiouser.

Pearl II was tearing around in Susan's backyard with an azalea bush she had uprooted. Hawk and Susan and I were having an entirely delicious sangria, which I had made, and eating cheese with French bread and cherries.

"What am I going to do," Susan said. "She uproots my shrubs, eats my flowers, digs huge holes."

"I could shoot her," Hawk said.

"Shush," Susan said. "She'll hear you."

"Just a thought," Hawk said.

He held out a small slice of cheese, and Pearl came to inspect it. She sniffed carefully, took it gingerly in her soft mouth, chewed it once, and spit it out. She looked at it intently for a moment and then rolled on it.

"I was thinking she might just eat it," Hawk said.

"That would be common," Susan said.

"Maybe she needs more exercise," I said. "Tire her out."

"I run with her every morning along the river," Susan said. "And Ann takes her to the woods at noon and lets her run with the other dogs. And Susanna comes around four and walks her for an hour."

"And she's not tired," I said.

"Not tired enough," Susan said.

"Ah, sweet bird of youth," I said.

"You're both making light of this, but I love my yard, and she's ruining it."

"She'll outgrow it," I said. "She's just a puppy, albeit a large one."

"Baby Hughie," Hawk said.

"I know," Susan said. "But by that time, I'll be living in a patch of arid waste-land."

"When this Emily Gold thing is over, maybe she can come stay with me for awhile," I said.

"That's Daryl's mother?"

"Yes."

"Did you find out anything useful at Taft?"

"Maybe," I said.

"Was Hawk with you when you went to Taft?"

"We're inseparable," I said.

"I read in the paper that there was a shooting," Susan said.

I smiled at her and nodded. She looked at Hawk. He smiled at her and nodded. Susan sat quietly for a moment, without anything showing in her face except being beautiful.

Then she said, "What did you find out?"

I told her. Pearl had discarded the azalea bush and was now digging intensely near the back steps.

"You mean Bunny Lombard gave an address now occupied by this Karnofsky person?"

"If Bunny is the same as Bonnie," I said.

"Did he live there when she gave the address?"

"Don't know yet," I said. "But among the things Sonny told me to lay off of was his family."

"You think she's his family?"

"Don't know yet."

Susan watched Pearl dig. I knew she was deeply distracted, because she didn't tell Pearl to stop.

"I assume that Karnofsky made another attempt at Taft," Susan said.

I nodded. The hole Pearl was so industriously digging was now deep enough to contain all but her rear end.

"And it hasn't deterred you."

"It has increased my anxiety," I said.

"Really?" Susan said. "I'm not certain you feel anxiety."

"I try not to dwell on it," I said.

"But you are frightened sometimes."

"Of course."

She looked at Hawk. "Are you ever scared?" she said.

"Ah is descended from generations of proud warriors," Hawk said.

"Oh, God," Susan said. "You're not going to give me some kind of Shaka Zulu rap, are you?"

Hawk grinned at her.

"All of whom were scared," he said.

"Like you?"

"Sho'."

Pearl came over smelling of fresh earth and put her head on Susan's lap. Susan stroked her automatically.

"But . . . ?" she said.

Hawk and I looked at each other.

"When I was boxing," I said, "people would occasionally say to me, 'doesn't it hurt to get hit like that?' And of course it did. But if I couldn't put up with the pain, I couldn't be a fighter."

Susan nodded.

"I know," she said. "You've explained it before."

"Repetition is an excellent learning tool," I said.

"Of course, I'm not talking about you,

anyway," Susan said.

"I know."

"I'm scared, and I don't want to be."

"You get used to it," I said.

"I wish I didn't have to," Susan said.

I shrugged. "I can't sing or dance," I said.

"I know."

Pearl moved over to Hawk and pushed her head under his hand to be patted.

"You folks barely talk," he said, smoothing Pearl's ears. "One of you say something cryptic, the other one say, 'I know.' Pretty soon you be speaking in clicks."

Susan smiled at him. "Yes," she said softly.

"Nobody gonna kill us," Hawk said.

"They never have," Susan said.

38
♦ ♦ ♦ ♦ ♦

So far it was a good day. No one had attempted to murder me. The weather was bright and pleasant. I had finished Tank McNamara and was reading Arlo and Janis. There was two-thirds of a large coffee and a second corn muffin beside me on my desk. Hawk, with a sawed-off doubled-barreled shotgun next to him on the couch, was reading a book about evolution by Ernst Mayr. I had the window open behind me, and the bright summer air smelled clean coming in.

When I finished Arlo and Janis, I called Rita Fiore at her office.

"I need a favor," I said.

"Your place or mine," Rita said.

"Not that kind of favor."

"It never is," Rita said. "What do you want."

I told her.

"Easy," she said. "I'll send a paralegal up to Essex County."

I thanked her and hung up and broke off half of my corn muffin. Suddenly Hawk dog-eared his page, put down his book, and picked up his shotgun. My office door opened. It was Epstein with a thin black leather briefcase under his arm. Hawk put the gun down and picked up his book. Epstein glanced at Hawk, glanced at the sawed-off, came to my desk, and sat in a client chair.

"That Hawk?" Epstein said.

"Yes."

Epstein turned in his chair.

"I'm Epstein," he said.

Hawk nodded. Epstein turned back to me.

"Malone was part of a surveillance team on Sonny Karnofsky, back in the early seventies, when the bureau was trying to put Sonny away."

"Anyone else on the team?"

"Malone was the youngest. Everyone else is dead."

"So he knew Sonny," I said, "from a long time ago. That's true of almost everyone in the cops-and-robbers business in Boston."

"It's better than finding out he didn't know him."

"They ever get Sonny?"

"No. But from what oral history I've been able to collect, Malone was occasionally seen in Sonny's company."

I nodded.

"That's all I have on Malone. Clean record. No hint of impropriety."

"How about Sonny?" I said.

Epstein took a folder out of his briefcase and opened it.

"Born Sarno Karnofsky, no middle name, in Hamtramck, Michigan in 1925. Married Evelina Lombard in 1945. Had a daughter, Bonnie Louise, born 1945. Did street-thug work in Detroit in the early forties, moved here the same year his daughter was born. You want his rap sheet?"

I shook my head.

"Worked here for awhile with Joe Broz, then split with Broz and, by 1965 had his own outfit," Epstein said and grinned. "The rest is history."

"Only in America," I said. "You got anything else salient?"

"Abner Fancy," Epstein said. "That salient enough?"

I could hear him struggling to keep the self-satisfaction from his voice. And failing.

"What about Abner?" I said.

"Did time in Massachusetts. Cedar Junction. Armed robbery."

"When?"

"Was in from 1961 to 1965."

"It was Walpole then. When did he get out?"

"What month?"

"Yeah."

Epstein looked into his folder. "Paroled February second," he said.

"So he had a PO."

"He did, but we can't find him. For crissake, Spenser, this was nearly forty years ago."

"Got the parole board hearing records?"

"In the folder," Epstein said. "Seems to have been a model prisoner."

Epstein put the folder on my desk. "You know anything salient I should know?"

"You know everything I know," I said.

"Let's keep it that way," Epstein said.

"You bet," I said.

Epstein glanced at Hawk without saying anything, hesitated for a moment, then left.

Without looking up from his book, Hawk said, "Liar, liar, pants on fire."

"I never got in trouble keeping my mouth shut," I said.

"Sonny got a daughter named Bonnie whose mother's maiden name was Lombard," Hawk said.

"I thought you were reading."

"Super Bro," Hawk said. "I can read and listen."

"It would be a spectacular coincidence,"

I said, "if Bonnie Louise Karnofsky were not Bunny Lombard."

"If Sonny live there back then."

"I'm working on that," I said.

"Rita?"

"Yeah."

"You ought to give in to her one time," Hawk said.

"And tell Susan what?"

"Line of duty," Hawk said.

I shook my head. "Maybe you need to step in," I said.

"Man, I got to do everything for you?"

"Almost," I said.

39

According to his prison sheet, Abner Fancy had been born out of wedlock in Boston in 1940. He was living in the South End when he was arrested, on Canton Street in the years when it was somewhat less rarified. There was no indication in the record that he was a problem while he was doing his time. The parole board, when they paroled him, took note of the fact that he had taken every class he could in the Taft prison-outreach program and appeared serious in his attempts to improve himself.

While I was reading Abner's folder, Rita Fiore called me.

"House at Seventeen Ocean Street in Paradise was purchased in 1961 by Sarno and Evelina Karnofsky for one hundred twelve thousand five hundred dollars," she said.

"Bada bing," I said.

"Bada bing?"

"Bada bing!"

"I gather this information is useful to you," Rita said.

"It is," I said.

"So you owe me?"

"I do."

"I want lunch," Rita said.

"I could send some over," I said.

"I want to eat it with you, you sonova bitch, so I can ply you with strong drink until you succumb."

"Oh hell," I said. "Everybody does that."

"Monday," Rita said. "Noon. Lock Obers."

"A debt is a debt," I said.

"You are one sweet-talking dude," Rita said and hung up.

"Bonnie is Bunny," I said to Hawk, "is Bonnie Louise Karnofsky."

"Sonny live there early enough?"

"Bought the place in '61."

"And when his daughter goes to college, she don't want to be the daughter of a hooligan," Hawk said. "So she use her mother's maiden name."

"And either Bonnie got morphed into Bunny," I said. "Or Daryl remembered it wrong."

"So where is Bonnie/Bunny now?" Hawk said.

"Alumni directory still has her living with Sonny," I said.

"She'd be how old now?" Hawk said.

"Late fifties," I said.

"Christ, how old is Sonny?"

"Late seventies," I said. "I have to do all the math for you?"

"I concentrating on saving your life," Hawk said. "Can't do that and math, too."

"You're easily confused," I said. "We could go out and ask her whereabouts."

"Sure," Hawk said. "Sonny be glad to tell us."

"Okay, so we put that plan on hold," I said. "She must have had friends in college. Maybe I can find one that's kept in touch."

"Lotta phone calls," Hawk said. "Could have Epstein pick her up for questioning."

"If he can find her," I said. "Fifty's kind of old to be living at home. And if he does find her, he hasn't got anything to hold her on. And if she has got something to hide, as soon as Epstein lets her go, Sonny will ship her off to Zanzibar, and nobody will find her."

"We could stake out the property," Hawk said. "See if we see her."

"We could," I said.

" 'Course, if we don't see her, it won't mean she isn't there," Hawk said. "Just mean she hasn't come out while we there."

"And if we do see her, how will we know

it's her," I said.

"And maybe Sonny a little more alert to stakeouts than your average suburban dad," Hawk said.

"And since he's trying to kill us anyway . . ."

"There you go saying 'us' again."

"All for one and one for all," I said.

"Don't that suck," Hawk said.

40

We settled for a lot of phone calls.

Of the 3,180 students that entered Taft in the fall of 1963, 954 of them were from greater Boston. The alumni directory had addresses for 611. At the rate of one minute per phone call, it would take me ten hours to call them all. If I didn't go to the bathroom. On the assumption that she would have more girlfriends than boy-friends, I went through the list again and winnowed out 307 female names.

"You wanna make some of these calls?" I said to Hawk.

"No."

"Maybe I'll be lucky," I said. "Maybe she was pals with Judy Aaron."

"You got one chance in three hundred seven," Hawk said.

"I thought you didn't do math."

"I do when I want to," Hawk said.

"They'll chisel that on your headstone," I said.

I picked up my cordless phone and leaned back and put my feet up and began.

Most of the calls took longer than a minute. Who was I again? Why did I wish to locate Bonnie Lombard? Was I authorized by the university? This was compensated to some extent by the people who hung up on me or who weren't home. Still, I'd been at it almost three hours when I talked to Anne Fahey.

"Bonnie? Sure, I remember Bonnie."

"May I come and see you about her," I said.

"Sure. You got my phone number, does that mean you got my address?"

I read her address to her.

"That's it. When do you want to come?"

"I'll be there in an hour," I said.

"Okay," she said. "Maybe I can rummage around, find some pictures or something. Should I do that?"

"Anything you have would be helpful," I said.

Anne Fahey lived in Sudbury, in a very large house of the kind that Susan called McMansions. There were Palladian windows and a number of roof peaks and an assortment of architectural conceits, all overlooking a vast lawn devoid of ornamentation.

Anne herself was a handsome woman in her fifties, with a lot of curly silver blond hair and a strong, graceful body. I introduced myself.

"And this is Mr. Hawk," I said. "My driver."

Hawk would be more easily mistaken for Santa Claus than someone's driver, but Anne smiled widely as she held the door open, as if she were unaware of my small deceit. We went into the front hall and then to the living room on the left. It appeared that, having spent far too much for the house, they had nothing left to furnish it. There were no rugs on the floor. There was a couch and three armchairs in the living room. The windows were undraped. There were no pictures on the walls. The huge slate-framed fireplace was ash-free, soot-free, and perfectly clean. There was nothing on the mantel. I sat on the couch. Hawk sat in an armchair with a view out the front window. Anne offered coffee. We declined.

"I found a few pictures of Bunny Lombard," she said.

"So her nickname was in fact Bunny?" I said.

"Yes. While I was waiting for you, I checked our yearbook."

She picked up a thick, white leatherette yearbook from the floor beside her chair. It read TAFT 1967 in blue script on the cover. Bunny had not stayed to graduate, so there was no individual head shot. But she had been in the drama club and the Sigma Kappa sorority, and she appeared in a group photo of each. There was also a candid of her at some sort of picnic, a very young woman wearing a tie-dyed T-shirt, her long dark hair cut straight across her forehead in bangs.

"That's me," Anne said, "with her. The one with the huge cup of beer."

She had been plumper then, with a big head of frizzy blond hair.

"I did a lot of beer in those days," Anne said. "Among other things."

"And now?" I said.

"A martini with my husband when he comes home from work."

"Adjusted to your environment," I said.

Anne grinned. "That would be me," she said. "Adjustable Annie. If people were eating smoked worms for supper, I'd be gobbling them right down."

"Nothing wrong with flexible," I said. "Did you know Bunny well?"

"Yes. We were both into causes. Did a lot of marches and sit-ins. Very serious. Smoked a lot of dope together, but very seriously. It was a political position to smoke dope then."

"How fortunate," I said.

"Yes. I notice as I grow older that if you have deeply felt political convictions, you can make pretty much everything fit them, if you need to."

"Yes," I said. "I've noticed that, too. She have any pet causes?"

"Mostly what we all had. The war! The establishment! The moral imperative of acid! She and I and about four other kids formed a prison outreach group. We figured all prisoners were political prisoners."

"Tell me about that," I said.

"We used to go down to Walpole two nights a week and give seminars on revolutionary politics with one of the professors."

"Whose name was?"

"Nancy Young."

"Do you know where she is?"

"Probably dead. She must have been in her fifties then. Big woman with a lot of gray hair. In retrospect, she was probably a lesbian. But we didn't think about that much at the time."

"How about the folks in charge at the prison," I said. "They didn't mind you teaching revolution to the inmates?"

"They thought we were just teaching American history. Nobody ever monitored us. We loved it. We thought we were revolutionaries. We decided to organize with some of the prisoners. Make a cell to help them when they got out or if they escaped. Like an underground railroad."

"What fun," I said.

"It was heaven," Anne said. "We wanted to help them escape, but we didn't really know how, and we never freed one. But several of them joined us when they got out. We felt so authentic, we nearly wet our pants."

"Can you remember who the prisoners were?"

"One of them called himself Shaka. We loved that. Shaka. It was so primeval."

"Can you remember his real name?"

"We would have called it his slave name in those days."

"Can you remember?"

"It was a funny name. Made me think of a comic strip."

"Abner Fancy?" I said.

"Yes, that's it. Abner Fancy. Always made me think of Li'l Abner."

"Any other prisoners?"

"There was another man, a friend of Shaka's, I think. We called him Coyote. I really can't remember his actual name. I probably never knew it."

I looked at the yearbook pictures for another minute.

"How about Emily Gold?" I said. "Any pictures of her?"

"Emily? Oh God, Emily. She was killed a long time ago. Murdered."

"Was she in your group?" I said.

"Yes. She was Bunny's best friend."

"She was in the group with Shaka and Coyote?"

"Yes."

"When did you last see any of these people?"

Anne was thumbing through the yearbook.

"Oh, God. Years. I'm a nice Irish Catholic girl from Milton. Once there were actually ex-convicts in the Brigade, I got scared. My only close friends in the Brigade were Bunny and Emily. They both dropped out of school, and I didn't. We just sort of drifted apart."

"Brigade?"

"Yes, we called ourselves the Dread Scott Brigade. D-r-e-a-d, isn't that so college kid?"

She pointed at a picture in a montage of photos.

"Oh, sure," she said, "here's Emily."

She looked like Daryl. Her hair was sixties straight, and she had the funked-out sixties look in a granny dress, but it could have been Daryl with a protest sign. The picture was too small for me to read the sign.

"And now she's been dead for . . . what?"

"Twenty-eight years," I said. "Her daughter looks just like her."

"She had a daughter? I didn't even know she was married . . . listen to me — as if she would have had to be married to have a child. God, am I middle-aged suburban or what?"

"It happens," I said. "Do you know where Bunny Lombard is now?"

"No idea," Anne said. "When I knew her, she was from the North Shore someplace. Paradise, maybe."

"When did you last see her?"

"She left in the middle of sophomore year, so 1965, I guess, probably in the winter. Why are you looking for her?"

"I wanted to ask her about Emily Gold," I said.

"Because of the murder?"

"Yes."

"I thought she was shot, like at random, by some guy holding up a bank."

"We'd like to find out who that was," I said.

"Are you working for Emily's daughter?" Anne said.

"I am."

"Jesus Christ," Anne said. "How are you going to find out a murder that happened twenty-eight years ago."

"Diligence," I said.

She smiled and shrugged. "Well," she said. "You found me."

41

It was a little after 3:30 in the afternoon when Hawk and I carefully opened up my office for a new business day. Hawk looked around the empty room.

"Harvey don't show me shit," Hawk said. "I working for Sonny, you be dead now."

"You wouldn't work for Sonny," I said.

"Beside the point," Hawk said.

I opened the windows behind my desk and looked out at the Back Bay. There was a group of three young women, rigorously conforming to the current look: cropped T-shirt, low-slung jeans, and a clear view of the navel. None of the three was slim enough to carry it off. Most people weren't. I listened to my messages. While I listened, Hawk unlocked my closet door, got the sawed-off, put it beside him on the couch, put his feet up on the coffee table, and began to read some more about evolution. I called Samuelson.

"Remember Ray Cortez?" he said.

"Leon Holton's PO," I said.

"Well, Ray appears to be a man of passionate convictions," Samuelson said. "He knows Leon is swimming in an ocean of drug money, and he seems to be getting away with it, and Ray's dying to violate him right back inside."

"I got no problem with that," I said.

"None of us do," Samuelson said. "After I got Leon's address from him, he started thinking more about Leon, and how last time Leon did time it was for possession with intent and he served nine months in Lompoc."

"Minimum security?" I said.

"It's like serving nine months at Zuma Beach," Samuelson said, "on a conviction that usually carries serious time, and even more so if it's your third strike."

"Third?" I said.

"Yeah. We got him for two, but Cortez says that Leon used to brag how he did time back there."

"In Massachusetts?" I said.

"Yep. He was bragging how connected he was."

"Back here?"

"All over. He said even if he got busted, he did soft time and not for long."

"Who's he wired to?" I said.

"I was wondering that, too," Samuelson said. "Which set me wondering why the

FBI queried us about him in '75. So I called the L.A. office. I get along with the SAC. And they checked back in the files, and it took them awhile but they found it. The request came from the Boston Office."

"Evan Malone," I said.

"I'll be damned," Samuelson said. "It always amazes me when you know something."

"Me too," I said. "They know why he wanted information?"

"No. They reminded me that it was twenty-eight years ago."

"Anything else bother you?" I said.

"Like, why did they query us?" Samuelson said. "Why didn't they query San Diego?"

"My question exactly," I said.

"That's scary," Samuelson said. "Anyway, I called a guy in San Diego, and he checked into it and called me back and said they got the same query."

"Any reason?"

"None on file."

"So they weren't sure where he was," I said.

"But they thought he was in Southern California," Samuelson said. "I checked San Jose and Oakland, where I can call in favors, and they got no record of any query on Leon Holton."

"So they were looking for him," I said.

"I'd guess," Samuelson said.

"But it wasn't an arrest query."

"No. Just information."

"So what'd they want?" I said.

"I've done all I can for you," Samuelson said. "You'll have to ask them."

"Thanks for your help."

"I'm not doing you a favor," Samuelson said. "Leon the Coyote is ours now, and I'd like him out of circulation."

"To protect and serve," I said.

"And kick some ass," Samuelson said. "When we can."

42

"Leon Holton spent five years in Walpole for attempting to rob a liquor store on Dorcester Avenue in 1960," Quirk said.

We were sitting in his office. Quirk had one foot up on an open file drawer in his desk. The crease in his tan flannels was still intact. His blue-and-tan-striped tie was loosened. His blue oxford shirt was open at the neck. His blue blazer hung wrinkle-free on a hanger on a hat rack near the door. Quirk thumbed through the thin manila folder for a moment.

"Paroled February second, 1965," Quirk said.

"Coincident with Abner Fancy," I said.

"Who the fuck is Abner Fancy?" Quirk said.

I told him about Shaka and about nearly everything else I had. He listened without speaking.

When I was done, he said, "The fucking Bureau."

"My thought exactly," I said.

"They're hard to fight," Quirk said.

"Maybe," I said. "But I think Epstein's with us."

"I know Epstein. He's straight, but he's a career guy in the Bureau. He can't do too much without blowing his career."

"I know."

"Which is why he's using you," Quirk said.

"I know."

"Me too," Quirk said.

"I know," I said.

"So where are you going to go from here? You got more info than the Census Bureau, and you still got no fucking idea what went down in that bank twenty-eight years ago?"

"If I could find Bonnie Karnofsky," I said, "I bet she'd know."

Quirk's door opened, and Belson came in. He looked at me.

"I saw Hawk outside with the motor running," he said. "I thought you might be sticking up headquarters."

"That would be big money," I said.

Quirk said, "Sit down, Frank, we need to think some stuff through."

Belson took the other chair. He was thin with a blue beard shadow that was always there no matter how recently he had shaved.

"Run it past him," Quirk said. "The short form, so I don't have to listen to it all over again."

I brought Frank up to date, omitting a few things as I had with Quirk, such as the shootout at Taft. Belson was motionless while I talked, looking straight at me, listening completely.

"Okay," Belson said when I finished. "You got Abner and Leon at the same joint where Emily and Bonnie are teaching revolution to the cons. At the same time, they are part of the Dread Scott Brigade. Nine years later, the Dread Scott Brigade claims credit for a bank stickup in which Emily is killed. Best we can tell there was a black guy and a white woman in the stickup. There was probably someone with a car outside. You have to figure that Emily wasn't in there to cash a traveler's check."

"I'm flattered," I said. "You listened."

"Be crazy to think all this ain't part of the package," Belson said.

I knew Belson wasn't talking to me. He was simply thinking out loud. Belson was perfectly okay at thinking, but his real strength was looking at a crime scene. He missed absolutely nothing. In his head, I knew he was trying to recreate what I'd told him into some pattern he could look at.

"Why are the Feds covering up?" Belson said.

I said nothing. Quirk prompted him.

"What do they usually cover up?" Quirk said.

"Informant."

Quirk and I both nodded.

"They had an informant in there," Belson said. "And when it went bad, they didn't want anyone to know that an FBI informant was participating in a bank robbery, while he . . ."

"Or she," I said.

". . . was on the payroll."

"So, assuming Frank's right, who's the informant?" Quirk said.

"Would they have covered it up if it were the vic?" Belson said.

Quirk smiled without warmth. "Sure," he said.

"Of course, we don't know they're covering up an informant," I said.

"They're covering up something," Belson said.

"And we'd like to catch them at it," I said.

Quirk and Belson both smiled.

"We would," Quirk said.

"Then we might as well work on the assumption that they were papering over an

215

insider operation that went sour," I said. "It could be Emily, or Abner, or Leon, or maybe Bunny."

"Or someone we never heard of," Belson said.

"Hey," I said. "It's your fucking premise."

"Emily's dead," Quirk said. "We got no idea where Abner is. We know Leon's in L.A., but he's not talking, and we got no leverage on him. We need to find the Karnofsky broad and pry her away from her old man."

"We got no leverage there either," Belson said.

"Yeah, but she's local and so are we," Quirk said.

"And after we've done that," I said, "then we need to get her to tell us what she knows and testify to it."

"Step at a time," Quirk said. "First we find her. Then we get her away from Sonny."

"I'm not sure there's a legal way to do that," Belson said.

Quirk grinned at him. Quirk's grin was but slightly less formidable than Quirk's glare. He jerked his head at me.

"That's what Private Shoofly is for," he said.

"You're suggesting some quasi-legal activity for me?" I said.

"B and E," Quirk said. "Kidnapping, forcible restraint. That sort of thing."

"And if it all goes to hell and the FBI slaps the cuffs on me?" I said.

Quirk smiled the smile again. "Then we do what, Frank?" he said.

"Deny any knowledge," Belson said.

"Cool," I said.

43

Paul brought Daryl to see me at the office. She looked uncomfortably at Hawk when she came in. But Hawk made many people uncomfortable. He didn't offer to leave, and I didn't ask him to.

"I," Daryl started. "I . . . need you to, ah, report."

"Sure," I said.

"I mean, I know I didn't really pay you much. Exactly."

"You paid me six Krispy Kreme donuts," I said. "That's a lot."

"Could you please tell me what you've learned?"

"Sure," I said.

I told her. She sat frowning with concentration.

When I got through, she said, "Do you mean that my mother was involved in the robbery?"

"Maybe," I said.

"And the Leon that my mom was fucking was a con?"

"Seems so," I said.

"And Bunny is the daughter of a gangster?"

"Yes."

She sat limply in the chair with her face sagging and didn't say anything.

"Can you question Bunny?" Paul said.

"We can't find her yet. If her father's got her hidden, she'll be hard to find."

We were quiet. Hawk had finished Ernst Mayr and was reading something called *Einstein's Universe*. I looked closely. His lips were not moving. It was bright outside, and the sun made long parallelograms on my floor. Daryl looked at me, and then at Paul, and not at Hawk. Then again at me.

"This isn't what I wanted," she said.

I nodded.

"I wanted you to get the bastard that shot my mother."

"I know," I said.

"You saw my father," she said. "How'd you like to grow up with him?"

I saw Hawk glance up from his book and almost smile for a second. Then he went back to reading.

"I don't want to know all this shit about my family," Daryl said.

"I don't blame you," I said.

"Why do I have to know this?" she said. She was leaning forward in her chair

219

now with her clenched fists pressed against her thighs, as if to keep them apart. Paul sat beside her with his face set in silence.

"Can't put it back," I said.

"I know that. Don't you think I know that? I don't want to know any more. I want you to stop. I'm going away."

"Where?" I said.

Paul answered. "Baltimore," he said. "Our run's over here."

"And I don't want to hear any more about this," Daryl said. "Okay? No more."

"You don't have to hear any more," I said. "But stopping is a little harder."

"Why would you keep doing it, if I don't want you to?"

"I guess because I sort of have to," I said. "There are too many hornets, and they're too stirred up."

"Hornets? Why are you talking about fucking hornets?"

I saw Paul set his face a little tighter.

"Since I started this thing," I said, "people have tried to kill me on two occasions."

"But why?"

"I don't know exactly, but it has to do with investigating your mother's death."

"How can you be sure?"

"And on two other occasions, people

have warned me to stop investigating your mother's death."

"They said that?"

"There are several people, it seems, that have pressing reason to want your mother's murder left unsolved. They aren't going to take my word, or yours, that I've stopped."

Daryl sat and stared down at her clenched fists. She shook her head slowly.

"I don't want this," she said. "I don't want any of this."

Nobody said anything.

"I don't want this," she said again, her head down.

"Daryl," Paul said. "This isn't just about you anymore."

She stood up suddenly.

"Well, fuck you," she said. "Fuck all of you."

And she turned and marched out of my office. Her swift passage made dust motes hover momentarily in the sunny rhomboids splashed across my office floor. Hawk dog-eared the page and folded his book shut.

"Fuck all of us?" he said. "What'd I do?"

"Wrong place, wrong time," Paul said.

"She's probably angriest at her mother," Susan said.

We were in a new restaurant called Spire. Susan was barely drinking a Cosmopolitan.

"I would have said she was angriest at me," I said.

"You were handy," Susan said. "Her mother died on her and left her to be raised by her hippie-dippie father."

"And she was probably angry at the person who killed her mother and left her to be raised by the hippie-dippie dad," I said.

"But she also, I suspect, wanted you to reinforce the fantasy she'd created."

"That if her mother hadn't been killed, the fantasy childhood would have been true."

"Maybe," Susan said. "Remember *The Great Gatsby*. . . . James Gatz's imagination had never really accepted his parents?"

"So," I said, "he invented just the sort of

Jay Gatsby a seventeen-year-old boy would be likely to invent."

"And to that conception," Susan said, "he was faithful to the end."

We were quiet for a moment. I was drinking a Ketel One martini on the rocks with a twist. It was nearly gone. Out of the corner of my eye, I located the waitress. Didn't want to wait until it was all gone. She met my eye. I nodded at the near-empty glass. She smiled and nodded, thrilled to serve me, and scooted toward the service bar. I looked at Susan.

"And?" I said.

"She changed her name," Susan said.

"Lot of actresses do that."

"If her name had been Lipschitz, that would make sense. She might have taken her mother's name, of course. Young women sometimes do."

"Gold," I said.

"And Silver is close."

"But still not the same," I said. "Let's assume you're right? Why hire me?"

"I would guess," Susan said, "that she hired you to enhance the family history, which she invented."

"And the opposite happened," I said.

"Something like that."

"Her mother was consorting with a convicted felon. Maybe part of a criminal enterprise."

Susan nodded.

"You ruined it," she said.

"But she knew when she hired me," I said, "that the fantasy childhood was false."

"People often know things that are mutually exclusive."

I saw the waitress coming with my second martini. I finished off the first, so as to round everything off nicely.

"I still can't just walk away," I said.

"No," Susan said. "You can't."

I looked at her across the table. Nobody looked quite like Susan. There were women as good-looking, though they were not legion, and there were probably women who were as smart, and I just hadn't met them. But there was no one whose face, carefully made up and framed by her thick, black hair, glittered with the ineffable femaleness that hers did. She was informed with generosity and self-absorption, certainty and confusion. She was subtle and literal, fearless, hesitant, objective, bossy, pliant, quick-tempered, loving, hard-boiled, and passionate. And it all melded so perfectly that she was the most complete person I'd ever known.

"What are you thinking about?" she said.

I smiled at her. "What would be your guess?" I said.

"Oh," she said, "that."

"In a manner of speaking," I said.

"Could we finish dinner first?"

"I suppose we have to," I said. "If we ever want to eat here again."

45

The Registry of Motor Vehicles told Quirk that Sarno Karnofsky had two Mercedes sedans and a Cadillac Escalade, registered in Massachusetts. Quirk told me and gave me the plate numbers. I had the three numbers written on a piece of paper taped to my sun visor as Hawk and I sat in my car with the motor off and the windows open to let the sea breeze in. Hawk had parked his car beside me and come to sit in mine. We were in a parking lot along with maybe fifty other cars, at a public beach, on the mainland end of the causeway that connected Paradise Neck with the rest of the town.

"So we going to sit here," Hawk said, "until hell freeze over or one of Sonny's cars comes off the Neck."

"Exactly," I said.

"And then we follow the car until we find Bonnie."

"Right," I said.

"You think that'll work?" Hawk said.

"I have no idea," I said.

"So why we doing it?"

"Because I don't know what else to do," I said.

Hawk was wearing black Oakley sunglasses and a white silk T-shirt. He watched a tanned young woman in a small black bathing suit walk toward the beach.

"That be your version of Occam's razor," Hawk said. "I'll do it because I don't know what else to do."

"Occam's razor?" I said.

Hawk shrugged, his eyes still following the woman in the meager bathing suit.

"I read a lot," Hawk said.

I nodded. The young woman sat down on a blanket near another woman in an equally insufficient bathing suit.

"You got a better suggestion?" I said.

"No."

"Then you agree we might as well do this."

"Yes."

An overweight woman wearing flip-flops and one of those two-piece suits with a little skirt walked by. She was pale-skinned. Her stomach sagged. Her hair was very blond and very teased. We watched her pass.

"The lord giveth," Hawk said, "and the lord taketh away."

"Have you ever thought we might be guilty of sexism here," I said.

"Yes," Hawk said.

A silver Mercedes sedan cruised past us, coming from the Neck. We checked the plates. It didn't belong to Sonny.

"For all you know," Hawk said, "Bonnie moved to Scottsdale twenty years ago to work on her tan."

"Sonny's going to all this trouble to cover her up," I said. "He might want her close."

"Or he might want her far," Hawk said.

"Well, yes," I said. "That too is a possibility."

"So we could be wasting a lot of time."

"Remember Occam," I said.

To watch the causeway, we had to sit with our backs to the ocean. But we could hear it and smell it and feel the breeze coming off it. Across the causeway, we could see the harbor, where the masts of the pleasure boats stood like marsh reeds. Herring gulls wheeled and squawked and got into a loud scrum over a remnant of hot dog roll on the edge of the street in front of us. A red Porsche Boxster went by with the top down. A slate gray Lexus SUV came by in the other direction. Then nothing. Then, after awhile, a blue Subaru Forester.

"Probably a servant," Hawk said.

228

"Can't be sure," I said. "The Yankees are a thrifty lot."

A black BMW came by, and a dark brown Mercedes sedan. Wrong license number. We could smell hot dogs cooking in the snack bar in back of the beach house. At 2:30, Hawk took action.

"Want a hot dog?" he said.

"Two," I said. "Mustard and relish."

"Want to pay for it?" Hawk said.

"No."

Hawk nodded. "Irish are a thrifty lot," he said, and moved off toward the stand.

We had eaten our hot dogs and drunk our coffee and taken turns at the men's room in the beach house. An Explorer and a couple Volvo wagons had gone by. An unmarked police car with a whip antenna pulled into the parking lot and stopped behind us. The driver got out and walked toward the car. He was a young guy, medium-sized, built like a middleweight boxer, moved like an athlete. He wore a short revolver on his belt and handcuffs and a badge. He came to the car on my side.

"How you doing," he said.

I nodded to indicate we were doing fine.

"My name's Jesse Stone," he said. "I'm the chief here in Paradise."

He didn't look like a small-town cop.

Something about the eyes and the way he walked.

"Nice to meet you," I said.

Behind his Oakleys, Hawk did not appear to be looking at Stone.

"You been sitting here since seven-thirty this morning," Stone said.

"Pretty good," I said. "You picked us up fast."

"We got a nice little department here," Stone said. "I don't wish to intrude, but what are you doing?"

"My name's Spenser," I said.

"I know. We already ran your plates."

"I'm trying to locate Sonny Karnofsky's daughter, Bonnie," I said. "There's a state cop named Healy can probably vouch for me."

"I know Healy," Stone said. "He still doing vice?"

"He never did vice," I said. "He's at One Thousand Ten Commonwealth. Homicide Commander."

Stone smiled slightly. "Why do you want Bonnie Karnofsky?"

"Long story," I said. "The short version is we think she's a witness in a murder investigation."

Stone nodded. "You want coffee?" he said.

"Sure," I said.

Without speaking, Hawk held up two fingers. Stone smiled again.

"Cream and sugar?"

"Both," I said.

"I'll be back in a couple minutes," Stone said.

He walked back to his car.

"He ain't no small-town shit-kicker," Hawk said.

"I know."

Stone reached into his car through the open side window, took out the radio mike, talked for a couple minutes, and put it back. Then he strolled toward the snack bar. While he was gone, five cars crossed the causeway, none of them registered to Sonny. In a few more minutes, he came back from the snack bar carrying three cups of coffee in a cardboard carrying tray. Balancing the coffee comfortably, Stone got in the backseat, sat, and distributed the coffee.

"Healy tell you I was everything a crime fighter should be?" I said.

"No. He said you'd probably do more good than harm."

"Ringing endorsement," Hawk said.

Stone nodded at Hawk. "He said you should be in jail."

"Nice of you to check," Hawk said.

With a pocket knife, Stone cut a little hole in the plastic lid of his coffee cup. He drank some coffee.

"Tell me the long story," Stone said.

I told him the story, editing out the shooting at Taft. He listened soundlessly. Three more cars passed us on the causeway. None of them Sonny's. When I was through, Stone stayed quiet for awhile, drinking his coffee.

"Sonny hasn't got her," he said finally.

"You know that," I said.

"Yeah."

"You know where she is?"

"No."

"How do you know she doesn't live with Sonny?" I said.

"Sonny's lived here awhile; we like to keep tabs on him."

"You've had him under surveillance?" I said.

"Yep."

"Has he spotted you?"

"Nope."

"How are you doing it?"

"One of his neighbors is a good sport," Stone said.

"You're in a house."

"Yep."

"You do camera surveillance?" I said.

"Yep."

"You have any pictures of Bonnie?"

Stone drank some more of his coffee. He seemed to like it. Another car went fruitlessly by on the causeway.

Then he said, "Yep."

46

I was in Stone's office at the Paradise Police Station. Hawk was still at the causeway. On Stone's desk were four somewhat grainy black-and-white head-shot blowups of a middle-aged woman. They weren't great pictures, but Bonnie was fully recognizable in them.

"So how come you never found out where she lived?" I said.

"No reason."

"Did you get her license number when she visited?"

"Sonny always sent a car for her."

"And you never followed her?"

"I got a twelve-man force," Stone said. "The surveillance is voluntary. We're lucky to get him covered as much as we do."

I nodded. On top of a file cabinet there was an expensive and often used Rawlings baseball glove.

"Sonny's daughter would have been about sixteen when he bought the house."

Stone turned one of the head shots toward him and looked at it for a minute.

"That would make her, what, fifty-seven?" Stone said.

"Somebody must have known her."

"You'd think," Stone said.

"She go to school here?"

"Don't know," Stone said. "I can find out."

"And find out if anyone knew her?"

"Probably," Stone said.

"Without getting Sonny all worked up," I said.

"I got the impression Sonny was already worked up," Stone said.

"I don't want him to bury her where I'll never find her," I said.

"According to Healy, that would have to be pretty deep."

"Wow," I said. "He likes me."

"I wouldn't go that far," Stone said.

I shrugged. We were quiet for a moment, looking at the photos on the desk.

"You ever do business with the Bureau?" I said.

"FBI?" Stone said and smiled. "Yes."

"What do you think?"

"I think a lot of the agents could have used more street time."

I nodded.

"You've had some," I said.

"Yep."

"Where?"

"L.A."

"You know a homicide guy named Samuelson out there?"

"I know the name," Stone said. "I worked for Cronjager."

"Don't know him," I said.

I took out one of my cards. "You learn anything, let me know," I said.

Stone took my card and slid it under the corner of his desk blotter. Then he picked up the photographs and slid them into a manila envelope.

"Take these along," he said. "I got more."

"Thanks," I said.

"Be my pleasure to bag Sonny," Stone said. "I don't like him."

I started for the door. Stone followed me.

"You being alone," Stone said, "I'll tail along back to the causeway."

"How kind," I said.

"Sonny murders you in my town," Stone said, "it'll fuck my chances for a pay raise."

47

♦ ♦ ♦ ♦ ♦

I was at the Hotel Meridian with Susan, at a fund-raiser for Community Servings, which was, like me, a nonprofit to which Susan was devoted. Hawk was with us, leaning against the wall, monochromatic in black and no more noticeable than a machine-gun emplacement. I myself was everything the date of a prominent psychotherapist should be: unobtrusive in a dark blue suit, dark blue shirt, pale blue silk tie, and a pair of sapphire cufflinks that Susan had given me to celebrate my virility. Susan was amazing in red silk and painful shoes. There were hors d'oeuvres in quantity, an open bar, and an ice-sculpture fountain from which flowed free and endless martinis. This seemed a great invention to me, and I felt privileged to have seen it.

The evening was called Life Savor and, in addition to Hawk, it drew a celebrity crowd. I spotted Oedipus, who was the program director for the big rock station in town and admitted to no other name. Will McDonough was there, and Bobby Orr, and Bill Poduska, the helicopter guy, and Fraser Lemley. I talked with Mike Barnicle and David Brudnoy. I was introduced to Jenifer Silverman, who assured me she was not related to Susan. I chatted with Chet Curtis. The Mayor came by, and a candidate for governor. Susan was on the board of this organization and raced around the room, greeting people and charming the ass off anyone lucky enough to be in her path. For a moment, that person was me.

"If the atmosphere gets any more rarified," I said, "I may get a nosebleed."

"Don't get any on my dress," Susan said and zoomed across the room to talk with Honey Blonder.

I pushed through the crowd to the martini fountain, and, in the spirit of participation, had a martini. Hawk kept me in sight. He was entirely unthreatening. To the extent that he had an expression as he moved through the crowd, it was one of benign amusement. But people made room for him. Hawk never had to fight for space.

I plopped an olive in my martini and took a sip. I said hello to Joyce Kulhawik. She moved on to talk with Emily Rooney and I found myself in eye contact across the crowded room with Harvey. I smiled at him, and he shot me elaborately with his forefinger, cocking his thumb carefully as he aimed and bringing it down when he fired. Then he looked past me at Hawk. The benignity was gone from Hawk's face. In its place was the stare. Hawk had never seen Harvey and maybe didn't know who he was. But Hawk knew what he was.

The two of them looked at each other for a long time. Harvey met the stare, which, redirected, might have frozen the martinis. I unbuttoned my suit coat. I checked the room to see where Susan was. If anything transpired, I wanted her out of range. The room was crowded, and I couldn't see her. Hawk's jacket was unbuttoned, too. He moved gently along the wall toward Harvey. I moved around the fountain toward Harvey from the other side. Harvey smiled and drew his forefinger across his throat and made a spitting gesture with his mouth. Then he moved through the crowd away from us and disappeared. Hawk looked at me. I shrugged. Not a good place to shoot it out. Hawk nodded and leaned on the wall again. I went and leaned beside him.

"What do you think?" I said.

"He ain't no fund-raiser," Hawk said.

"Name's Harvey," I said. "Sonny's hired gun."

"He still think he going to scare you off?" Hawk said.

"I doubt it."

"So why you think he's here?"

"I don't know," I said. "You got a theory?"

"He's a freak," Hawk said. "He like shooting people."

"He's not going to shoot me here," I said.

"No," Hawk said. "This be foreplay."

I scanned the room for Susan and spotted her talking with Bob Kraft. Good.

"That makes sense," I said.

"It do," Hawk said. "He giving himself a little thrill, come here, flirt with you. Go home. Think about it. Make his night."

"Usually, it's women," I said.

Hawk smiled. "Sometimes you got to settle," he said.

48

I was at my desk with pictures of Bonnie Karnofsky spread out on my desk. Hawk and the shotgun were settled in together on my office couch. Hawk was drinking coffee and reading the *New York Times.* I was drinking coffee and looking at the photos. In her adulthood, Bonnie was pretty good-looking, in a blonde, big-haired kind of way. However, information crucial to any decision of how good-looking she was had been omitted. The blown-up photographs were only of her face. They were useful for identification purposes only.

The phone rang and I answered.

"Hi," a woman said. "I'm officer Molly Crane from the Paradise Police. Chief Stone asked me to call and give you some information."

"Shoot," I said.

"Be careful what you say to an armed officer of the law," she said.

"Ill-phrased," I said. "What have you to tell me?"

"Bonnie Karnofsky did not attend any

school in Paradise," she said.

"Do you know where she went?"

"School department shows only that it was an accredited private school."

"I'm sure Taft will probably have it in their admission records," I said, so she wouldn't feel she'd failed.

"Very likely," she said. "Chief Stone also asked me to tell you that we have built a file on Sarno Karnofsky, which Chief Stone has examined since he talked with you."

"And?"

"And he thinks you might find it interesting. Do you have a fax?"

"I do."

"If you will give me your fax number," she said, "I will fax you as much of the file as Chief Stone thinks relevant to your investigation."

"That's very kind," I said. "But why didn't Chief Stone give me this stuff when I was there?"

"Chief Stone didn't speak of it," she said. "But I would hazard that he wanted to reexamine the files himself and perhaps get further bona fides on you before he turned over secret surveillance material."

"You got a nice little department there," I said.

"We do. May I have your fax?"

I gave her my fax number, and in about five minutes the machine rang and the material began to creep out of it. I waited until it was all out, and then assembled it and read it through twice.

"I know," I said to Hawk, "that you are a simple lout with a gun, placed here for my protection."

Without looking up, Hawk said, "Yassah."

"But," I said, "I have come across some things which could actually be clues, and I was wondering if I might share them with you."

"Long as you don't use no big words," Hawk said and put the newspaper in his lap.

"Mrs. Sarno Karnofsky, the former Evelina Lombard, has her own phone, separate from her husband's," I said.

"Sounds like the first step toward open marriage," Hawk said.

I ignored him.

"Seems that several times a week she makes a phone call to a phone belonging to Sigmund Czernak," I said.

"See," Hawk said. "She got something going on the side."

"Mr. Czernak resides in Lynnfield," I said.

"Somebody got to," Hawk said.

"Further underscoring the theme of independence," I said, "is the fact that Mrs. Karnofsky has her own bank account, separate from her husband's."

"Maybe I wrong," Hawk said. "Maybe independence be the secret to a happy marriage."

"How happy would you be if you were married to Sonny?"

"If I was me?" Hawk said. "I be miserable."

"I mean if you were a woman."

Hawk grinned. "I be miserable," he said.

"Every month," I said. "Mrs. Karnofsky wires two thousand dollars to the La Jolla Merchants Bank to the account of Barry Gordon."

"Daryl's father?"

"Yep."

"Goddamn," Hawk said. "That maybe do sound like a fucking clue."

"Maybe two," I said.

49

"I met a friend of yours today," Susan said.

We were at the bar at Mistral, contributing quietly to the hubbub. On the other side of Susan, Hawk had caught the attention of a stunning young woman in a very small black dress, and they were talking deeply.

"Really?" I said.

"Yes. He said he'd seen me the other night at the Meridian, at Life Savor. Said to tell you Harvey says hello."

Hawk turned way from the girl in the black dress and looked at the room.

"Tall?" I said. "Kind of limp? Longish blond hair, suntan, blue eyes, a diamond stud in his ear. Funny sort of mouth. Like a shark?"

"Well, I never thought of the shark thing," Susan said. "But yes. How do you know him?"

I thought a minute about what to say, couldn't think of any way around it, and settled for the truth.

"He's not a friend," I said. "He's a button man."

"A what?"

"A hired killer," I said.

Susan frowned and didn't say anything for a moment. Then she said, "And he's letting you know he can reach me if he needs to."

"Yes."

"Is it the thing about Daryl's mother?"

"Yes."

The girl in the black dress was staring at Hawk's back in something like disbelief. What happened to their relationship?

"We can kill him," Hawk said.

"And maybe we will," I said. "But there'll be someone else."

"We could kill Sonny," Hawk said.

"And maybe we will," I said. "But he's hard to get to, and who watches Susan while we do?"

"Maybe you should consult Susan," she said.

"We should," I said.

"I have always known the downside of loving you," Susan said. "And there's so much upside that it is well worth it."

"I've been telling you that for years," I said.

She smiled. "And it makes me uneasy to hear you talk about killing people because someone said he knew you."

"You know what he meant," I said.

"I know what he said."

"I . . ."

Susan shook her head. "Not you," Susan said. "Me. It's what I want. I'm the one that was threatened."

"What do you want?"

"I'm scared," Susan said. "I can't pretend I'm not. And I want to be protected."

"You'll be protected."

"But," she said, "I also know that you can't kill everyone who threatens me. How many might there be?"

"There might be a fair number," I said. "There's a lot of people involved in ways I don't know yet."

"So you need to finish up this case," Susan said.

"I can walk away from this case," I said.

"I know you would," Susan said. "But how would we feel if people could chase you off a case by implying a threat to me?"

I had no answer for that, so I gave none. Sometimes it's effective.

"I'll protect her," Hawk said.

"You're protecting him," Susan said.

"He can protect himself," Hawk said.

"Twenty-four hours a day," I said. "Seven days a week until it's over."

"I'll get a couple people to help me," Hawk said.

Behind him, the young woman in the scant dress paid her bill with a credit card and stalked out without looking at Hawk. I didn't ask him who he'd get or if they were good. If he got them, they'd be good.

"Quirk can talk to Cambridge," I said. "Have them put a car out front."

Hawk grinned. "There be some known felons coming and going," Hawk said. "Be sure they know that."

"I'll organize it with Quirk," I said.

"Could Vinnie go with you?" Susan said to me.

"If Vinnie's available, he'll go with Hawk," I said.

We were quiet for a short time. I watched Susan think.

"Yes," she said. "If one of us has to be unprotected, you are much more able than I am."

"Suze," Hawk said. "He much more able than anybody . . . 'cept maybe me."

50

Sigmund Czernak had a big tree-shaded white colonial house with a rolling lawn and a picket fence that faced the town common. On the common, in front of a white eighteenth-century meetinghouse, there was some sort of fair. Folding tables with baked goods. Balloons. A popcorn machine that perfumed the air all the way to Czernak's back door. I parked in the turnaround at the top of the drive, headed out, between a dark blue BMW sports car with a gray top, and a black Mercedes SUV. There was a dark blue Ford Crown Victoria parked beyond the Mercedes. I went around to the front door, walking under a maple tree that must have been older than the house, and rang the front doorbell. A small, white, ratty dog yapped at me through the screen door.

"Careful," I said to him, "I'm armed."

From somewhere behind the dog, a woman's voice said, "Sherry, quiet down." There were footsteps, and Bonnie Karnofsky appeared in the doorway. Sherry didn't quiet down. She yapped some more.

"Yes?" Bonnie said.

"Hello," I said. "My name is Spenser, and I'm looking for anyone who knew Emily Gold."

"Excuse me?"

I said it again.

"Who's Emily Gold?" Bonnie said.

"Your classmate at Taft," I said. "Remember, you and Emily and Shaka and Coyote?"

"You are talking ragtime," she said and raised her voice and yelled, "Ziggy."

She had far too much blond hair, which would probably abrade the skin if you brushed against it. But her face was youthful and pretty, and her body was quite aggressive in tan shorts and a yellow tank top. A man appeared behind her, tall and slender with back hair slicked back tightly to his skull and big horn-rim glasses. The ratty little dog was yapping steadily.

"Who's this," he said to Bonnie.

"Guy asking questions," Bonnie said. "I don't know what he's talking about."

"Whaddya want, Jack?"

"I'm trying to locate people who knew Emily Gold," I said.

"We know any Emily Gold?" he said to Bonnie.

"Never heard of her," Bonnie said.

"So fuck off," he said to me.

"That was great," I said. " 'Fuck off.' Wow! You don't much hear talk like that anymore. It made my knees weak."

"Bunny," he said to Bonnie. "Get Harry."

She disappeared. Ziggy froze me with his stare. The dog yapped. It wasn't getting anywhere, but it wasn't losing ground either. Two men appeared behind Ziggy.

"Him," Ziggy said. "Asking Bunny questions."

The two men pushed past Ziggy and opened the screen door and came out onto the front step with me. The fresh popcorn smell drifted across the front lawn from the common. One of the men was wearing a flowered Hawaiian shirt unbuttoned over his undershirt. He pulled one side of it back to let me see that he was wearing a gun.

"Eek," I said.

"No rough stuff here," Ziggy said. "Take him somewhere."

"We could go to the fair on the common," I said.

"Look at that, Cheece," the guy in the Hawaiian shirt said to his pal. "He ain't scared."

Cheece was a thick dark man with a

Vandyke beard and small eyes kept barely apart by the bridge of his flat nose.

"Yet," Cheece said.

He took hold of my left arm and started to steer me away from the front door. "We'll go around back," he said. "Then we'll see."

"Sure thing," I said and pulled my arm away. "No need to push."

I set out ahead of them toward the back of the house where my car was parked. The two of them had to hurry to stay a step behind me. At the corner of the house, I turned right, and as Cheece came around the corner, I turned and hit him full out with a right cross that snapped his head left and put him on his back. As he rounded the corner, the guy in the Hawaiian shirt reached for his gun. I caught his right wrist before he could get to the gun and pulled him toward me and turned him so that I could bend his arm up behind his back. I put my left forearm under his chin and put some pressure on his neck. Then I turned both of us so Hawaiian Shirt was between me and the house. He was between me and Cheece, too, but Cheece was just now beginning to sit up, and I knew that his chimes were still ringing. It was Ziggy and whoever else was in the house that I needed to think about now. I began to back toward my car, dragging Hawaiian Shirt with me. He didn't make a sound. As I was halfway across the driveway, I saw Ziggy appear in the back door. He looked at Cheece, who was now on his hands and knees, and at Hawaiian Shirt and me in the driveway. He disappeared from the back door for a moment and then reappeared carrying what looked like a 9mm semiautomatic, though it could have been a .38- or a .40-caliber. If he shot me with it, the difference would be insignificant. I was at my car. I kept my left forearm tight on Hawaiian Shirt's throat and let go of his right arm and pulled my own small gun. I poked it into Hawaiian Shirt's back so he'd know I had one.

"You stand right there or I will shoot you to death," I said.

I let go of his throat. He didn't move. With him still screening me and my gun still pressed against his spine, I reached behind me with my left hand and opened my car door.

"Stay right there," I said and slid in to my car and put the key in, starting the engine. From around the jamb of his back door, his body mostly screened, Ziggy was aiming at me with both hands on the gun. Still holding my gun, I put the car in drive and floored it. The car lurched forward, tires screaming with friction as they spun on the hot top driveway. Hawaiian Shirt hit the ground the minute the car moved, and a bullet thumped through the backseat passenger window of my car. I bent as low as I could as I tore down the driveway. I felt, more than heard, another bullet tear into the body of the car somewhere. Then I was out of the driveway and onto the street and gone, only a little worse off than I was before.

51

♦ ♦ ♦ ♦ ♦

Ty-Bop and Junior were sitting on the front steps of Susan's house when I pulled up in front. They looked at me with recognition but no warmth. They were both black. Junior was about the size of Faneuil Hall, and Ty-Bop was average height and thin. They worked for Tony Marcus: Junior the muscle, Ty-Bop the shooter. I didn't care for them. I didn't care much for their boss, if it came to that. Even so, I nodded at them as I went up Susan's front stairs. Neither one nodded back. Churlish.

Pearl greeted me with an exuberant lunge, and when I went into the hall, I squatted and endured her exuberance until it abated. Hawk stood in the door of Susan's study, across from her office, and watched. When it was over, I stood and went past him into the study and sat on the couch against the front wall below the window.

"Ty-Bop and Junior?" I said.

"Tony owed me," Hawk said.

"Ty-Bop's about nineteen," I said.

"He older than he look," Hawk said.

"Okay, so maybe he's twenty," I said. "He's also a cocaine addict."

"He won't use while he's working here," Hawk said.

"You spoke to him," I said.

"I spoke to him. I spoke to Tony."

I nodded. "How about they're scaring the crap out of everyone on Linnaean Street," I said.

"That's a bad thing?" Hawk said.

"No," I said. "Susan seen them?"

"Yes."

"And?"

"Any friend of mine," Hawk said.

I nodded again. "Okay," I said. "As long as you trust them."

"They'll stay," Hawk said. "Tony's word is good."

"Got anybody else?"

"Vinnie'll be back in town tomorrow," Hawk said. "Cambridge puts a cruiser out front at night from eleven to seven. And, if all else fails, we got you."

"Not for a couple of days," I said. "I gotta go back to San Diego."

"Barry Gordon?"

"Yes. Can you arrange a gun?"

"Just like last time," Hawk said. "How about Bonnie/Bunny? You find her?"

"I found her."

"And?"

I told him.

"Figure the husband's in the family business?"

"Seems so," I said. "And he or his father-in-law or both of them don't want anyone talking to Bunny."

"Or at least don't want you," Hawk said. "You thought you could waltz in there and chat her up?"

"I was counting on charm," I said.

Hawk grunted. "Maybe we need to get her out of there," Hawk said. "Get her someplace quiet where your charm can do its work."

"We may have to," I said. "Let's see what I can shake loose from Barry. What time is Vinnie due?"

"Be here tomorrow morning," Hawk said.

I looked at the closed door of Susan's office.

"She got a client?" I said.

"Woman," Hawk said. "In a short skirt."

"Observant," I said.

"A natural gift," Hawk said.

A client canceled, and Susan had a two-hour break before the next one. We had lunch together upstairs in her apartment. I told her what I knew and what I was going to do.

"People are going to some lengths," Susan said.

"And I'm not quite sure why," I said.

"It must have something to do with that bank robbery when Daryl's mother got killed."

"But what?" I said. "Was she there? Did she do the shooting? Is there something else?"

"Do you think Barry Gordon knows?"

"He knows something worth two thousand dollars a month to Bunny's mother."

"And you can't call him on the phone?"

"Can't scare him as effectively on the phone," I said.

"You plan to scare him."

"Yes. I can't pay him more than Mrs. Karnofsky."

"Can you scare him more than Mr. Karnofsky?" Susan said.

"A guy in your living room is more scary than a guy three thousand miles away," I said.

We were sharing a large tossed salad and hot cornbread, which I had put together while I waited for Susan. Susan nibbled on a wedge of purple heirloom tomato, which we had bought on Sunday at

258

Verrill Farm. She nodded.

"And," I said, "we don't know for a fact that Sonny, Mr. Karnofsky, knows about the money going to Gordon."

"Because it comes out of her bank account," Susan said.

"Yes."

"But wouldn't he be the one putting money into the account?"

"Doesn't mean he knows how she spends it," I said.

"No," she said. "I suppose it doesn't."

I ate a square of cornbread. Susan had a bite of red lettuce. In a move reminiscent of her predecessor, Pearl coiled in and around our feet — ever hopeful.

"How do you feel?" I said to Susan.

"Being in danger is rarely pleasant," she said. "And though the prospect of being in danger without you is less pleasant, I'm feeling well looked-after."

"How do you feel about Junior and Ty-Bop?"

"They're hideous," Susan said. "But I trust them because Hawk said I should."

I nodded. "Vinnie will be along tomorrow," I said.

"Vinnie is not actually charming," Susan said.

"That's because you haven't seen him

259

shoot," I said.

"And I hope not to."

We finished our lunch, during which I gave Pearl a couple bites of cornbread when Susan wasn't looking. The second time, she caught me.

"You are just teaching her to beg from the table," she said.

"If she's going to do it," I said, "isn't it best if she knows how?"

Susan pretended that what I said was not amusing. "Oh, God," she said.

In the afternoon, Susan saw the rest of her patients while I organized my travels. That night, we had supper together and went to bed early. Unfortunately, Pearl went to bed with us, which is a bit like trying to make love around a giraffe.

We are, however, experienced, determined, and adroit.

We managed.

52

On a case where I'd been paid six Krispy Kreme donuts, air travel alone had put me in deficit. But here I was again in San Diego with a Colt Python loaner gun and a rented Ford Taurus, driving up Route 5 again, toward Mission Bay to visit Barry Gordon. It was warm and sunny and pleasant in San Diego, as it always was, except when it was warm, rainy, and pleasant.

The Lab was lying in the sun on the front step when I arrived at Barry Gordon's little house. He didn't bark this time. Maybe he remembered me. Or maybe he was too comfortable in the sun to bother. I reached down and scratched him behind the ear before I knocked on the door.

Barry said "Hey" when he opened the door.

I said "Hey" in return and shoved him back into his living room and shut the door behind me.

"Whaddya doing, man?" Barry said.

I walked to him until my chest was

against his and my face was maybe an inch from his face, if I bent my neck.

"Hey, man," Barry said. "What the fuck?"

"Barry," I said. "You have been bullshitting me."

"Like hell."

"I hate it when people bullshit me."

"I never bullshitted you, man."

"Why does Evelina Karnofsky send you money every month?" I said.

"I don't know who that is, man. Honest to God."

I slapped him with my open right hand across the face. It was hard enough to make him stagger two steps sideways. He put his forearms up on either side of his face.

"I didn't do nothing," he said. "I didn't do nothing."

"This can get a lot worse, Barry. Tell me about Evelina Karnofsky."

"I can't, man. I don't know nothing. . . ."

I hit him again. His forearms were still protecting his face, but the blow rocked him sideways again and scared him more than it hurt him. He doubled up with his hands clasped over his head.

"Evelina?" I said.

He didn't say anything. It was hard to slap him, doubled up like he was, so I punched him lightly in the left kidney. He fell. I hadn't hit him hard enough to knock him down. He was on the floor now, his arms around his head, his knees up, trying to curl into a ball.

"Evelina?" I said.

He stayed where he was. I gave him a friendly kick in the side.

"Evelina?"

"Stop it. Don't kick me. I'll tell you. Stop it."

"Sure," I said.

I reached down and helped him up. Upright, he stayed bent over as if he'd been shot in the stomach. Lucky, I hadn't hit him hard. He'd have probably died.

"I need to sit down," he said.

"Sure."

"Gimme a minute, man, lemme get myself together."

"Take your time," I said.

When necessary, one could play good cop/bad cop alone.

He sat and started to make himself a joint. His hands were shaking. The left side of his face was red where I'd slapped him. He got the joint assembled. And lit. And he took a deep, long drag on it and held it in as long as he could before he exhaled slowly. He studied the burning end of the joint for a moment. Then he leaned forward a little and put his elbows on his knees and looked straight at me.

"Daryl ain't really my daughter," he said.

"She know that?" I said.

"No."

"Tell me about it."

"I don't know all about it," Barry said. "Just the part I know about, you know?"

"Tell me that part," I said.

He took another long drag on the reefer. "Me and Emily was living in a house downtown," Barry said, "with Bunny and a couple black dudes, a guy named Abner, and a guy named Leon."

He smoked some more.

"And Abner and Bunny kind of paired off. And me and Emily got together. And Leon was mostly bringing home, you know, the harlot of the night."

The joint was gone. He made another one, calmer now, his hands steady as he talked. I waited. He spent awhile getting the joint together and getting it lit.

"So who had the, ah, fling with Emily?" I said.

"Emily had a lotta flings," Barry said. He

was easy now, gliding on marijuana. "But that ain't what went down."

I nodded. Patient, but stern.

"Emily ain't Daryl's mom, neither."

Jesus Christ.

Barry knew it was headline news. He waited a moment to let the effect sink in, enjoying it. Feeling important. Feeling happy now, on his second joint.

"Tell me about that," I said.

"Abner and Bunny were going really hot and heavy," Barry said. "Her especially. She was like a bitch in heat around him."

He paused for a moment and smiled to himself, I think, remembering. I waited. He remembered.

Finally I nudged him. "Uh-huh."

He smoked some more and then came back to me. His smile was beginning to look a little loopy.

"And," he said, "anyway, he knocked her up."

"What was Abner's last name?" I said.

"I don't remember. It was a funny name."

"Dandy?" I said.

"No, man. But like that."

"Fancy?"

"Yeah. That's it. Abner Fancy. What a hot-shit name."

"And Bunny?"

"Like I tole you last time. When I knew her then, she was calling herself Bunny Lombard."

"But that wasn't her real name."

"No."

"Her real name was?"

"Karnofsky," Barry said. "Bunny Karnofsky. No wonder she changed it."

"Daryl is Bunny's daughter?"

"Her and Abner's," Barry said.

"So how did she end up with you?"

Barry grinned. A big grin, a high and happy grin. Forget about being slapped around. All is forgiven. He took a drag on his cigarette.

"Jesus," he said, his voice odd and strained as he let the smoke out through it slowly. "Where are my fuckin' manners? You wanna toke, man?"

"Thanks, no," I said. "How did Daryl end up with you?"

"Bunny gave her to us."

"Just like that?"

"Yeah. Baby was fair-skinned and, you know, Emily was dark anyway. No one was going to notice."

I walked to the door and looked out at the black Lab sleeping in the sun, on his side, his eyes shut, his tongue lolling out. I turned and looked at Barry.

"Why?" I said.

"Emily kind of liked babies," Barry said. "And, like, Bunny said she'd give us support money."

"Or her mother would," I said. "I was more wondering why she gave her to you than why you took her."

"She didn't want her."

"Any reason?"

"I don't know," Barry said. "Maybe she didn't want a shvartzeh kid. I think she just didn't want the bother. At least she didn't leave it in a Dumpster."

"Good for her," I said. "You adopt her?"

"Not really," Barry said. "But I got her birth certificate. In case anything ever came up."

"May I see it?"

"It's in a safe place."

"Safe from whom?" I said.

"Whoever," Barry said. His loopy smile had a crafty little edge to it.

"That's why the support payments keep coming," I said.

He shrugged.

"Even though she's thirty-four and gone," I said.

He shrugged again. The reefer had burned down to the most meager of roaches. He could barely hold it. Carefully, he took a last long drag on it, trying not to burn his lips.

"That's how you live," I said. "That's how you got this house. All that crap about her grandparents' insurance. You've been blackmailing Bunny for years."

"Two thousand a month ain't much," he said.

He snubbed the remnant of his reefer out in his ashtray and began to fumble with the makings for a new one.

"So she was yours for, what, six years, and then Emily took up with Leon, and then she got killed and . . ."

"The cops shipped her back to me, everybody thought I was her father," Barry said. "What the fuck, man, Leon wasn't going to keep her."

"You didn't need her for the blackmail scam," I said. "You had the birth certificate."

Barry shrugged. "She'd been with me for six years," he said.

I stared at him. The counterculture had always seemed Saran-Wrap thin to me. Passionate about abstraction, flaccid about human feelings. Barry was inarguably an aimless creep. But there it was. He'd taken Daryl and made some vague and nearly useless attempt at fathering her. I shook my head.

268

"What?" Barry said vaguely.

"Where does Leon fit in all this?"

"I don't know. He was fucking Emily for awhile, then she went away with him. Then she got killed. I don't know much about him after she got killed."

"He involved in that bank holdup?" I said.

"I dunno."

"He know about Daryl?"

"What about her?"

"Did he know she was Bunny's daughter."

"Naw. Me and Emily and Bunny was the only ones who knew."

"Abner didn't know?"

"Oh, him, yeah, I suppose."

"You know what happened to him?"

"Naw."

He had smoked himself past good feeling and was starting down the hill to depression.

"You know who Bunny's father is?" I said.

He started to cry.

"Naw, man. Shit, I don't know nothing. I never knew nothing. I never been nothing."

"Well, I guess you were Daryl's father," I said. "Sort of."

53

I was having breakfast with Captain Samuelson at Nate and Al's deli in Beverly Hills, just two booths away from Larry King. In the booth with us was a thin-faced, sandy-haired FBI agent named Dennis Clark. Samuelson said he had no reason to bring Leon downtown, and that Leon was known to be heavily lawyered, and in the current climate, Samuelson didn't want a black man's lawyer screaming publicly about police harassment.

"On the other hand," he said, "it would seem no more than courteous for us to go with you when you stop by for a chat."

"Reduces the chance that he'll shoot me, too," I said.

"I suppose it does," Samuelson said.

I had ordered scrambled eggs with onions. Samuelson had shredded wheat. Clark was drinking black coffee.

"I'm here because Epstein called me," Clark said. "We went through the academy together. He's a good agent and a good guy."

"We appreciate it," I said.

"Just remember, my presence is completely unofficial."

I nodded. Samuelson ate some of his cereal.

"We just need you to be there, Dennis," Samuelson said. "You don't have to say a word."

"Just so you know," Clark said.

"We know," Samuelson said.

"And if I swear I wasn't present, you both back me."

"We do," I said.

Clark looked at Samuelson.

"Of course, Dennis," Samuelson said. "Absolutely."

Clark nodded and drank his coffee. Samuelson sprinkled some Equal on his cereal and ate a spoonful.

"Why'd you decide to talk with him again?" Samuelson said to me. "You learned bubkes last time."

"I got the tacit admission that he knew Emily Gordon," I said.

"The broad that got killed."

"Yes."

"You knew that anyway."

"Well, yes."

"You learn anything else?"

"No."

"So why do you think you'll do

better this time?"

"Ever hopeful," I said.

"Ever a pain in the ass," Samuelson said.

"I value consistency," I said.

"Okay," Samuelson said. "We'll drive up and see him."

An L.A. police captain and an FBI agent got more respect at Leon's house than Hawk and I had gotten. We were ushered in without even a patdown by the same greeting team that Hawk and I had met. We went into the same ridiculous room, where Leon was waiting for us in the same chair. Today he was wearing a black-and-gold dashiki. He gave us the same pre-programmed stare.

Samuelson introduced himself and said, "I believe you've met Spenser."

Leon made one small nod to indicate that he had. It also indicated somehow that he hadn't been impressed.

"And this other gentleman," Samuelson said, "is Special Agent Dennis Clark of the Federal Bureau of Investigation."

Samuelson gave "Federal Bureau of Investigation" a nice dramatic overtone.

"Spenser and I are working in cooperation with the Bureau," Samuelson said solemnly.

"Yeah?"

"Old case," Samuelson said. "1974."

"Yeah."

"And, well, let's not beat around the bush," Samuelson said. "We know you're involved."

"Involved in what?" Leon said.

"The FBI has informed us that you were involved in a bank holdup in Boston in 1974 in which a young woman you were with was killed."

"Boston?"

"Uh-huh. The woman was Emily Gold, and we know she was your girlfriend. We're not sure you killed her," Samuelson said, "but the Bureau thinks you did, and they've asked us to talk with you."

"The Bureau thinks I killed some broad in Boston?" Leon said.

He was staring at Clark.

"Yep."

"Show me something, says you're FBI," Leon said.

Clark showed him a badge. Leon studied it. "You the one thinks I killed somebody in Boston?" he said to Clark.

Clark shook his head.

"So," Leon said to Samuelson, "who the fuck you talking to thinks I killed some broad."

"From the Boston office," Samuelson

said. "Special Agent Malone."

"Malone?"

"Yeah. Evan Malone."

"You're lying."

"Cops don't lie, Leon," Samuelson said. "You know that."

"He knows I didn't kill her."

"We can prove you knew her," I said.

"Malone knows I didn't do it, the lying motherfucker."

"How's he know that?" Samuelson said.

"I wasn't even in the fucking bank, man."

"Where were you?"

"I was just the driver, man. Malone knows that."

"How," Samuelson said.

"Man, I told him. He knows I didn't shoot that broad."

We were quiet for a moment. We had been right. It was as if we all knew it at the same time. The other two let me say it.

"You were the mole," I said.

"Huh?"

"You were the undercover guy. The informant. You were working for the Feds and Malone was your handler."

"Yeah."

Leon seemed calm about it. He still assumed the Bureau would take care of him.

"And when the bank job went down, they didn't want you compromised."

"Right."

I nodded.

"So who killed Emily Gold?" Samuelson said.

"I don't know, man. I tole you. I was in the car. They come busting out of the bank and said Emily got shot and to roll it."

"Who was in the bank?" I said.

"Shaka, Bunny, white hippie asshole I don't even remember his name, and Emily."

"Shaka was Abner Fancy?"

"Yeah. Sure."

"Emily go in with them?"

"No, I tole all this to Malone, for crissake. Emily was the scout. She go in ahead of time, case the place, and if she don't come out in three minutes, we go in. They go in. I just the driver."

"And no one ever said who shot her?"

"No, man. I figure it's some fucking cowboy bank guard, until I read the papers and they say it ain't known who shot her, and then Malone get me and ships me out of town."

Clark forgot his vow of silence.

"And set you up here?" Clark said.

"Yeah," he said.

Clark's face showed nothing.

"Where's Shaka?" Samuelson said.

"I don't know."

"How about the white hippie asshole?"

"He's dead."

"How."

"I heard Shaka shot him."

"Because?"

"Because he a fucking cokehead and he having a fucking miscarriage about the shooting in the bank."

"And Shaka thought he'd rat?"

"No harm being sure," Leon said.

"Except maybe to the white hippie asshole."

"How about Bunny?"

"Shit, man, I ain't seen Bunny since it went down."

"Weren't you her main squeeze?"

Leon shrugged.

"For awhile," he said. "She used to be Shaka's when he still Abner Fancy. Then he dump her for Emily, which leaves her on the loose. So Bunny's a pretty hot little bitch, and I scoop her for awhile. But I dumped her before the bank thing. I think she was having eyes for Abner again."

"Who was now Shaka," I said.

"Yeah. We was all big for names back then," Leon said.

"You know Emily had a husband?"

Leon smiled a very thin smile.

"I heard that."

"And a kid."

"Yeah. Daryl. I remember the kid. Emmy brought her when she took off with me."

We were quiet.

"What are you guys fucking around with this thing for now?" Leon said.

"Maybe so we can put you in the jug, Leon," Samuelson said. "And hammer in the cork."

"Me. You fucking can't touch me. I got a deal with the fucking federal government. Ask him, the FBI fuck." Leon pointed at Clark. "He'll tell you."

"You got no deal with me, Leon," Clark said.

"Fuck you. Ask Malone. You people can't touch me. We got a deal."

Nobody said anything.

"Okay. Arrest me or get the fuck out," Leon said. "I ain't talking no more without my lawyer."

Samuelson stood.

"We'll get back to you," he said.

And the three of us left.

On the ride back down the hill, with Samuelson driving, Clark said, "You know they weren't just worried about keeping Leon in place."

"I know," I said.

"They didn't want it known that one of their paid informants was the wheel man for a bank job," Clark said.

"I know," I said.

"I'll talk with Epstein, see if we got a chance. Maybe we can open this thing up and let a little air in."

"Maybe we can bust Leon, too," Samuelson said.

"I'll talk with Epstein about that, too," Clark said. "You know what it's like fighting the system you're in."

"I do," Samuelson said.

"It's why I'm not in one," I said.

"Really?" Samuelson said. "I talked about you with some people in Boston. They said you got canned for being an obstreperous hard-on."

"That's the other reason," I said.

54

I was home. More or less. It was evening, and I was in Quirk's office with Epstein and Quirk, entertaining them with tales of California.

"You think Leon would have blabbed like he did, if Clark wasn't there?" Quirk said.

"No. Leon sort of thought Clark would protect him. In twenty-eight years, he must have gotten pretty used to assuming the Feds would protect him," I said.

"So we know why the Bureau sat on this thing," Epstein said. "What we don't know is who killed Emily Gold."

"We could bring Bunny Karnofsky in and ask her," I said.

"On Leon's say-so?" Epstein asked. "Twenty-eight years later?"

"Capital crime," I said.

"Sure," he said. "And Sonny Karnofsky's daughter. They will have her lawyered up so tight we may not even be able to see her."

"And then she's on notice," Quirk said.

"And, my guess, she and her husband will take a long trip someplace and no one will be able to remember where."

"You know the husband?" I said to Quirk.

"Ziggy Czernak. He used to be one of Sonny's bodyguards."

"Now he's Bunny's bodyguard."

"Maybe it's true love," Quirk said.

"Maybe."

Quirk looked at his watch. "Late," he said. "My wife will be annoyed."

"You scared of your wife?" I said.

"Yeah. You going to tell the kid?"

"Daryl?"

"Yeah."

"That her parents aren't who she thinks they are?"

"Yeah."

"I don't know. I still need to find out who killed . . . the woman she thinks is her mother."

"Day at a time," Epstein said.

Outside Quirk's one window, the summer evening had settled in. It wasn't quite dark, but the sky had turned that navy blue and the color permeated the atmosphere. There were occasions when this was my favorite time of day.

"So, what do you want to do?" I said.

Epstein and Quirk looked at each other.

"I still have the home office to fight," Epstein said.

I nodded.

"Sonny's got resources," Quirk said. "I don't want Bunny to get scared off and disappear."

I decided not to mention that she might already have been scared off by me. I thought it best, for the moment, to assume that they'd leave her in place and try to bury me.

"We need to get Bunny alone," I said.

"We do," Quirk said.

"You have any suggestions?"

"You and Hawk could get her out of there," Quirk said.

"Excellent idea," Epstein said. "Unofficially speaking."

"Hawk's with Susan," I said.

Quirk nodded.

"I figure Frank and I could sit in on that as, ah, private citizens during off-duty hours."

"I could sit in on that," Epstein said.

"Unofficially," I said.

"Of course," Epstein said. "Unofficially."

"Be nice if we knew where Abner Fancy was."

"Would be," Quirk said.

"I wouldn't want you to exhaust your-selves," I said. "But have you looked?"

Quirk nodded.

"He's not in the system," Epstein said. "We don't know where he is, or even if he's alive."

"Well," I said. "When I get Bunny alone, I'll ask her."

"Let us know," Quirk said, "when you want us in Cambridge."

"I will," I said. "You'll get to meet the new Pearl."

"Is she calm and relaxed?"

"No," I said. "She'll bark and race around and, if she likes you, jump up and rest her paws on your shoulders and lap your face."

"I think I went out with her once," Epstein said.

55

The car picked me up as I turned onto Mass. Avenue going home from Police Headquarters. It was a dark burgundy Lincoln, and the driver was pretty good. He dropped back several cars behind me, changed positions occasionally, and once even turned off and went around the block, in a stretch where there was no chance for him to lose me. It's easier to tail at night, because mostly to the guy being tailed you're merely a set of headlights like every other set. But in this part of town, the streetlights were bright and the traffic was heavy, so the ambient light was pretty good.

The last time anyone had tailed me, the plan had been to shoot me. I assumed there was a similar plan in place now. It would be someone from Sonny, and, given how badly it had gone the last time or two, I suspected that this time it would be Harvey, the specialist. I could go around the block and back to Police Headquarters and probably discourage the stalker. But that would just postpone things, and something happening was more likely to resolve this mare's nest than nothing happening. The question was where to let it happen. I stayed on Mass. Avenue while I thought about this, through the South End and into the Back Bay. At Beacon Street, I turned left and, a block later, swung right up the ramp onto Storrow Drive. I drove west along the river into Allston and went up the slight ramp at the Anderson bridge, turning left away from the bridge onto North Harvard Street. A half block up, I turned right into the parking lot at Harvard Stadium and parked. I unlocked the glove compartment and took out the 9mm Browning I kept for emergency firepower. I ran a shell up into the chamber, let the hammer down, and got out and walked through the open doors into the nearly total darkness under the stands.

In less stressful moments, I had come here with Susan, who thought it a perfect conditioning plan to run up and down the stadium steps. I found it most effective in keeping my knees sore. I went up the entry stairs and into the moon-brightened area low down in the stands, close to the field.

Harvard Stadium was a bowl, open at the northerly end. At the top of the stadium was a covered arcade where people could circle until they found their seating section. With the Browning in my right hand, I went up the stairs on the run, grateful at this moment for the hours with Susan. It was still a long way to the top. I felt conspicuous in the bright moonlight. I thought of a line from Eliot . . . something about the nerve patterns displayed on the wall by a magic lantern . . . My back felt tight, I could feel a gun sight on it. I could hear my heartbeat and my labored breathing as I went up. I was wearing sneakers, but my footfalls still seemed blatant in the pale, empty stadium. No one shot me.

At the top I was in under the arcade roof, shielded by the chest-high wall. From where I stood, I could see most of the stadium. There was no movement. Harvey might not be a fan of the Crimson, and might not know the stadium as well as I did. He also knew I was in here, and he might proceed with caution. My throat was tight. My breath still rasped. Nothing happened. Where were they? I waited in the stillness and the moonlight. Nothing. I waited. Nothing. I waited. Across the stadium, I saw a figure rise cautiously from an entrance near the goal line. I looked below. There was another figure on this side.

There were at least two of them. In the gentle moonlight, it was hard to say for sure, but neither of them looked like Harvey, which meant he was somewhere else in the stadium. They wouldn't have sent anyone else, not after I had been to the Czernak home. Not after I'd actually spoken to Bunny. The men below were now fully out of their stairwells, crouching as they came. Both had shotguns. Swell. At the closed end of the stadium, behind the goalposts at the other end of the field, a third figure emerged from the stairwell. Even from where I was, I knew it was Harvey. I stayed where I was. The three men stood still now and slowly surveyed the stadium. Then they moved up a few steps and did it again.

I realized why they had been so long in coming. First they had swept the space under the stands, starting at either end and driving anyone there toward the middle, where Harvey waited. Now they were doing it in the stadium, working their way up, and if they found no one by the time they got to the top, they would move along the arcade toward the center, pushing anyone up there toward the center, where Harvey waited. It would not be good to let them do that. The guy across the way was a long shot with a handgun, probably one hundred yards. The guy near me would be duck soup. I cocked the Browning and stood in the shadow of one of the support posts. I rested my elbows on the top of the wall, and, holding the gun in both hands, I centered in so that the middle of the far man's body sat on top of the little gun sight at the front of the barrel. I centered the front sight in the V of the back sight and leveled it off. I took in some air and let it out and stopped breathing. I squeezed the trigger slowly and kept squeezing, firing five rounds. One of them got him, maybe more than one. He twisted suddenly and dropped the shotgun and fell forward. I didn't see him hit. I was on my feet, firing at the second man, close to me. He had no place to go. He sank to a knee between the seats and raised the shotgun and fell backward, and the shotgun fell on top of him. I looked for Harvey. He was gone. My ears rang. The silence of the stadium after the eruption of gunfire was almost more assaultive than the gunshots.

I was alone with Harvey now, in the thin moonlit darkness, to play another kind of game in the big arena. Fight fiercely, Harvard. He couldn't run. He couldn't go back to Sonny and say I'd killed the other two and chased him off. He'd played this game before and never lost. He thought he could kill me. I had four rounds left in the Browning and five in the Chiefs Special on my hip. I thought I could kill him.

I stood motionless and didn't breathe and listened. There were faint occasional traffic sounds from Soldier's Field Road. There was a barely discernable breeze. There might have been a hint of river smell in it. There was no sound or scent or sight of Harvey. What would I do if I were he? He knew where I was, or where I had been when I shot his pals. He'd have run toward me. He'd be in the arcade. I put the Browning on the edge of the wall and took out the .38 and cocked it and transferred it to my left hand. Shooting left-handed, I couldn't hit the ocean from a boat, but if Harvey were close enough . . . I picked up the Browning again. He'd expect me to stay against the back wall of the arcade so I wouldn't get shot from the stadium. I stayed instead against the front wall. He'd expect me to stay where I was. Instead, I moved in a crouch, keeping my head below the wall.

The stadium smelled like stadiums always smell — of peanuts, or popped corn, or both. I speculated that the Roman Coliseum had probably smelled of peanuts, or popped corn, or both. I moved slowly and very carefully, sliding each foot silently along, feeling for anything that might crunch underfoot and give me away. There was nothing. My compliments to Harvard Facilities Maintenance. I moved this way past two stair openings, with the Browning held straight out in front of me ready to shoot. If he had gone up where I'd last seen him and started carefully toward where he'd last seen me, we would meet pretty soon.

I was breathing through my open mouth as quietly as I could. I was listening and looking. The effort to perceive was physical. If I were not where he was expecting me, if only for a moment, that distraction would be my edge. Or not. I could hear small murmuring pigeon sounds and realized that they were nesting under the rim of the arcade. Somewhere one of the pigeons fluttered a little as if he were turning over in bed, and there was Harvey, crouching as I was, against the front wall, his gun half pointed toward the back wall. He turned the muzzle toward me and I shot him in the middle of the mass with the four bullets left in the Browning.

It had been enough edge.

56

Alone in my apartment on Marlborough Street, I sat at my kitchen counter with a tall Scotch and soda and cleaned the Browning.

I had just killed three men, two of whom I didn't even know. What kind of business was I in, where I had to kill three men on a pleasant moonlit night in an Ivy League football stadium. *Hope tomorrow isn't parents' day.* There had been two people at Taft awhile ago. If I shot anyone else on a college campus, I'd probably be eligible for tenure. I drank half my drink.

Sometimes the work helped people. But who was getting helped this time? Did Daryl want to know what I had learned? Would it help her? Was I the one to decide that? Several people had died so far in pursuit of information that no one might wish to acquire. They hadn't been good people. But I had known I'd have to kill them when I led them to the stadium, where I knew the layout and they didn't. I hadn't known there'd be backup. But I hadn't known there wouldn't be. Did I stick at it because I was curious? Because I was a nosy guy who wanted to know what everyone had been covering up? Now I knew. Or at least I knew most of it. Was it worth a lot of dead guys? I did this work because I could. And maybe because I couldn't do any other. I'd never been good at working for someone. At least this work let me live life on my terms.

I ran the swab through the barrel of the Browning, and it came out clean. I looked down the barrel. Spotless. I wiped the gun off with a cloth and let the receiver forward, let the hammer down, and had more Scotch. The nearly full half gallon on the counter gleamed reassuringly in the light from under my kitchen cabinets. I fed cartridges into the magazine of the Browning. They went in economically, each one taking no more space than it needed to. Nice-looking things, bullets. Compact. Bright brass casing, copper coating on the slug, leaving some gray lead exposed at the blunt nose. When it was loaded, I slid the magazine into the pistol butt.

My glass was empty. I made another drink and took it to the front window and looked out at Marlborough Street at 2:15 a.m. The brick and brownstone faces of the buildings were blank. No windows were lighted. The cars parked on the street seemed abandoned in their stillness, and the bleak street lamps made the street look lonelier than I knew it was.

I was doing this because I had started out to do this, and if you are going to live life on your own terms, there need to be terms, and somehow you need to live up to them. What was that line from Hemingway? *What's right is what feels good after?* That didn't help. I took a long drink of Scotch and soda. There was that line from who, Auden? *Malt does more than Milton can to justify God's ways to man.* I could see my face reflected in the window glass. It was the face of a guy who used to box — the nose especially, and a little scarring around the eyes.

I went back to the counter and sat and looked at the Browning 9mm semiautomatic pistol as it lay there. As an artifact, it was nice-looking. Well-made. Precise. Nice balance to it. Blued finish. Black handle. Everything it should be and no more than that. Form follows function. The magazine was full and in place. But there was no round in the chamber. As it lay on my countertop, it was less dangerous than a sixteen-ounce hammer.

Maybe Harvey lived life on his own terms, too. And maybe he was faithful to the terms. Maybe that was why he'd kept coming in the dark unknown stadium when both his backup were gone. What would he be doing tonight if he'd won? Was that the only difference? That it maybe bothered me more than it would have bothered him?

I took my drink with me and went around the counter and picked up the phone and called Susan. Her voice was full of sleep.

"Guess I woke you up," I said.

"It's quarter to three," Susan said. "Are you all right?"

"More or less," I said. "I needed to hear your voice."

The sleepy thickness vanished from her voice.

"Where are you?" she said.

"Home."

"Are you drunk."

"Somewhat," I said.

"Do you need me to come over?"

"No," I said. "I need you to tell me you love me."

"I do love you," Susan said. "Sometimes I think I have loved you all my life."

"You haven't known me all your life."

"A meaningless technicality," Susan said.

"I love you," I said.

"I know," Susan said. "Has something bad happened?"

"I've had to shoot some people," I said.

"You're not hurt."

"No."

"You've had to shoot people before. It's part of what you do."

"I know."

"But?"

"But," I said, "rarely in pursuit of so measly a grail."

"The truth?"

"The truth sometimes sounds better than it is," I said.

"I agree. But it's no measly grail."

"And the violence."

"You are a violent man," Susan said. "You have been all your life."

"How good a thing is that," I said.

"It's neither good nor bad," Susan said. "It simply is. What makes you who you are is that you have contained it within a set of rules that you can't even articulate."

"Sonova bitch," I said.

"You know it's true," she said. "Even bad as you feel right now, and some of that is booze talking, at the center of your soul you know you didn't do a wrong thing."

"Maybe that's a lie I tell myself."

"No," Susan said.

"Flat no?"

"I'm a shrink. I'm allowed to say that. Besides," Susan said, "you are the damn grail."

"I am?"

"You are," she said. "A lifelong quest to be true to who you are."

"And that's a good thing?" I said.

"It's the only thing," she said. "Good or bad. It is the simple fact of you." I could hear the smile in Susan's voice. "And for what it's worth, I wouldn't want you to be different."

"Even if I could be," I said.

"Which you can't," Susan said.

"So what makes me better than Harvey?"

"Would I ever fall in love with Harvey?"

"No."

I didn't say anything. Susan let me be quiet for awhile. Silence was never a problem for us.

"No," I said. "You couldn't."

"There's your difference," Susan said.

"I'm okay because you love me?" I said.

"No. I love you because you're okay."

Again we shared a silence.

Then I said, "Thank you, Doctor."

"Take some Scotch," Susan said. "Call me in the morning."

57

♦ ♦ ♦ ♦ ♦

"If we can get her alone," I said to Hawk, "I can get her to talk."

"Don't you know enough?"

"No. I need to know who killed Emily Gordon."

"You think you might be getting obsessive about this?" Hawk said.

"Susan says it's because I am my own grail."

"That's probably it," Hawk said. "But you already know more than the client wants to find out."

"I want to know," I said.

"Oh," Hawk said. "Long as you has a reasonable explanation."

We were drinking coffee in Hawk's car again in the parking lot at the end of the causeway in Paradise. It was a perfectly swell morning. The temperature was 78, the sun was out, the breeze was gentle. Behind us, the Atlantic Ocean was endlessly rocking. It was cool enough to reduce the number of exotic bathing suits. But in a fallen world, even perfection is flawed.

"What are we looking for," Hawk said, as a little silver Mercedes, the kind with the retractable hard top, drove past us toward the Neck.

"Whatever we can see," I said. "We're really here to think up a way to get Bonnie Karnofsky alone."

"Now that you've shot up everyone but Bunny," Hawk said. "So they won't be expecting anything."

"I haven't shot anybody named Karnofsky," I said.

"Yet," Hawk said. "You figure she's with Dad and Mom."

"Almost certainly," I said. "There's no sign of life at the house in Lynnfield. Whatever Sonny's protecting her from, he's running out of room. I'll bet my reputation that he's brought her home."

"You got no reputation," Hawk said.

"Okay, so it's not a risky bet."

"And don't we know what he's protecting her from?"

"Maybe," I said. "Maybe the murder. Or maybe he doesn't want anyone to know she's guilty of miscegenation."

"Like the founding fathers," Hawk said.

"But not the founding mothers."

"You don't know that," Hawk said.

"You mean there might have been a

Solly Hemings?"

Hawk grinned. "Probably my ancestor," he said.

I drank some more coffee. Nothing wrong with several cups of coffee. Stimulates the brain. If I drank enough of it, my brain got so stimulated that I couldn't sleep. But trying to think through a difficult problem . . . I'd be a fool not to use it.

"So how do we get to her?" I said.

"I dress up like Solly Hemings and walk back and forth past the house until she sees me, and, overwhelmed by desire, she dash out and we grab her."

I put my head back against the headrest. "We better think of a backup plan," I said. "In case that doesn't work."

"Sho 'nuff," Hawk said.

We finished our coffee. I got out and went to the snack bar and got us two more cups.

"We can go in and get her," Hawk said. "Or we can lure her out."

"Place is like a Norman keep," I said. "We go in, and a lot of people will get hurt."

"And we likely to be two of them," Hawk said.

"So how do we lure her out? Aside from the Solly Hemings ploy."

We thought about that for awhile. In front of the car, a squabble of gulls fought loudly over half an orange.

"We got her daughter," Hawk said.

"Even if she cares about her daughter, I can't do that."

"Use the daughter to trap the mother?"

"That's right."

"Man, you're confusing," Hawk said. "And not amusing. Couple days ago, you shot three guys. Now you won't use the daughter against the mother."

"I confuse myself sometimes," I said.

We drank coffee. The gulls squawked at one another. A Ford pickup went past us, toward town, towing a large sailboat.

"We gotta go in," I said.

Hawk took in a long breath and let it out slowly and didn't say anything.

"You know we do," I said.

"Uh-huh."

Two teenage girls in designer shades and miniscule bathing suits went past us, carrying beach bags and a blanket and a portable radio.

"Too young," I said.

Hawk nodded sadly. "I know," he said.

Our coffee was gone. Hawk went and got some. Keep drinking it. It was bound to work.

"The house backs up on the water," I said.

Hawk looked at me. His face brightened. "Think it got a private beach?" he said.

"If you had all that dough and owned that property, would it have a private beach?"

"It would."

"And if you were Bonnie Karnofsky Czernak and you were shut up in there with Mom and Dad, what would you decide, sooner or later, to do?"

"After I watched *The View*?"

"After that," I said.

"Might take my blanket and my radio and go down to the sea."

"Me too," I said.

"We need a boat," Hawk said.

"We need a lot of things," I said. "But at least we have an idea."

"Don't happen often," Hawk said.

"No," I said. "I'm surprised I recognized it when it came."

58

Hawk and I were with Jesse Stone in the town launch, which was throttled back and wallowing a little, one hundred yards off shore on the ocean side of Paradise Neck. The boat was being steered by the harbormaster, a heavy man named Phil who wore blue jeans and suspenders.

"That's Karnofsky's beach," Stone said.

He had on his chief shirt with his badge on it, jeans, a baseball cap, and sneakers. He carried a Smith & Wesson .38 with a short barrel, just like mine. The perfect choice. Hawk, ever self-amusing, wore a blue blazer and white pants, and one of those boating caps with the long bill, like Hemingway.

"Can we assume they've spotted us?" I said.

"Sure. But it doesn't matter. They're used to us coming by."

"That little gully runs straight up between the rocks to the top of the hill behind Sonny's house," Stone said. "Got aerial photos, you want them."

"I do."

Stone nodded.

"On the other side of the rocks, maybe two, three hundred feet," he said, "is neighboring property."

"How about the other side?"

"Further," Stone said. "Other side of that point. There's a right of way down to the water."

The harbormaster kept the nose of the boat into the waves, idling just enough to hold our position.

"They use the beach much," I said.

"Sonny, never. The old lady, some." I scanned the rocks and trees around the beach.

There was a raft with a springboard anchored fifty feet from shore.

"Their raft?" I said.

Stone nodded.

"They use it?"

"Daughter comes to visit sometimes. She and her husband use it."

"How deep is it by the raft?"

"Phil?" Stone said to the harbormaster.

"Twenty feet," Phil said. "Drops off pretty sharp from the beach."

We were quiet, while far out into the Atlantic beyond us some sailboats were swooping about, and a couple of fishing boats plodded into the wind. On shore, nothing moved except a couple small seabirds with long beaks, which poked around in the rocks without any visible result. I knew how they felt.

"How often do they use the raft," I said.

"We don't check it every day," Stone said. "But when the weather's good, she's down here. She bakes for awhile and then goes in and swims to the raft. I assume it's to cool off. Hubby goes sometimes. Sometimes doesn't."

"I don't suppose we can use your boat," I said.

"It's the town's."

"I still assume we can't use it."

"You can't."

"You don't talk much," I said. "Do you."

"It's an experiment," Stone said. "If I got nothing to say, I try not to say it."

"Maybe I'll try it sometime," I said.

"You got a plan?" Stone said.

"We off the record here?" I said.

"I look like a fucking TV crew?" Stone said.

"I'm planning to snatch Bonnie Czernak, née Karnofsky," I said.

"Good thing I'm not a fucking TV crew," Stone said.

"Where do you stand on that," I said.

"Off to the side."

"I'm not asking you to do anything but leave it alone," I said.

"I do that well," Stone said.

59

We set up on the other side of the point at the bottom of the path that formed the right of way. The Zodiac that Hawk had acquired bobbed on the gentle chop of the water that lapped the rocks in the shelter of the cove. Hawk and I had a picnic basket to explain what we were doing on the rocks if anyone came by. Though, in truth, Hawk didn't look that much like a picnic guy. But at the least it served to carry the bunch of sandwiches we'd bought at a takeout shop in Paradise. We had binoculars and a bird book to explain them, though Hawk didn't look much like a birder, either. I was watching Karnofsky's beach through the glasses, peering over the edge of the rock, while Hawk ate a roast beef sandwich and drank coffee from a Thermos.

"Can you actually drive that thing?" I said.

"Course I can," Hawk said. "Used one for a year once."

"Doing what?"

"Covert stuff," Hawk said. "In Burma."

"Everything you do should be covert," I said.

"This the third day we be here," Hawk said, "and we ain't seen nothing but some seagulls."

"I looked in that bird book," I said. "They are officially known as herring gulls."

"Hot damn," Hawk said.

He took another bite of his sandwich and another sip of coffee.

"Susan okay?" Hawk said.

"Yep. Quirk was there last night."

"What I like," he said, "is when I thinking 'bout Quirk marching over there to relieve Ty-Bop on guard duty."

"I'm just hoping Ty-Bop doesn't get a snootful of coke and shoot up West Cambridge."

"Ty-Bop be clean till we done," Hawk said. "How long we going to hang here?"

"Until she shows up or we think of something better," I said.

"That's how long I figured," Hawk said. "How's Susan taking to the security stuff."

"She's had to do it before."

"Kind of hard on her, ain't it."

"It is, but she thinks I'm worth it."

"Goddamn," Hawk said. "Think what I'd be worth."

"Hoo, hoo," I said.

"Hoo, hoo?"

"Here she comes," I said.

Hawk ate the last of his sandwich and finished his coffee. Then he turned onto his belly and snaked up the rock and lay beside me, looking over at Bonnie Czernak and her husband. They were in bathing suits. Bonnie carried a beach bag. The two men who came down with them set up a couple beach chairs for them. And they sat.

"That the husband?" Hawk said.

"Ziggy," I said.

"He sing reggae?" Hawk said.

"Not that Ziggy," I said.

Bonnie took a portable radio out of the beach bag and set it on the ground beside her chair and fiddled with it. In a moment, some rock music drifted over to us. Bonnie rubbed oil on herself and put opaque white shields over her eyes and lay back in her chair. Ziggy talked on his cell phone. The two bodyguards stood around under the trees and looked bored. Hawk and I lay behind the rock and took turns with the binoculars and were bored. Behind us, the Zodiac moved gently on its tether. The sun was clear and steady. The rocks were hot. On her reclining chair, her sun-dark skin slick with tanning oil, Bonnie fried in the sun.

"We don't get her pretty soon," Hawk said, "she be dead with melanoma."

"When she swims to the raft," I said.

"Burn, baby, burn," Hawk said.

At about quarter of three in the afternoon, when I was near turning into a barnacle, Bonnie stood, dropped her eye shields on the sand, walked to the water, splashed herself to get used to it, and then plunged in.

"Okay," I said to Hawk.

We slid down the rock and into the Zodiac. I hunched over the engine as if I were trying to fix it, and Hawk paddled us with one oar slowly around the rock and in toward the beach where Ziggy sat with the bodyguards. They'd seen me. But they hadn't seen Hawk, so I kept my face turned away, hunched over the engine, trying to get it started. Bonnie paid us very little heed as she swam toward the raft. She was a strong swimmer, and she looked good. But she kept her head up out of the water, so she wasn't much for speed. Susan swam the same way. It was about the hair.

"I think we're out of gas," Hawk shouted to the men on the shore.

"Well, this ain't a fucking gas station,"

Ziggy shouted back. He stayed seated. "Beat it."

"Just lemme use your cell," Hawk shouted. "I only got one oar. I can't row this sucker all the way around the Neck."

We were now between Bonnie and the shore.

"What part of fucking *beat it* don't you fucking understand," Ziggy shouted.

Bonnie pulled herself up on the raft and sort of rubbed the water off herself like Esther Williams. The two bodyguards came down to stand beside Ziggy and look menacing. One of them made a dismissive wave-away gesture. Hawk shrugged and turned the boat a little and began to paddle away, past the raft. He let the oar slip from his hand.

"Shit," he said loudly and stood up.

I stayed hunched over the big outboard. The motor had an electric start, off a heavy marine battery beneath it on the floor of the Zodiac. As we drifted next to the raft, Hawk stepped up onto it, picked up Bonnie around the waist, and stepped back into the Zodiac. I hit the electric start button and the motor roared and the boat jumped. Hawk fell over backward with Bonnie still clamped in his arms. On shore, the two bodyguards had their guns out but they couldn't shoot for fear of hitting Bonnie. Ziggy, too, was on his feet. He was yelling, and I think Bonnie was screaming, but the engine was too loud and I couldn't hear either of them.

60

Bonnie talked all the way from the point where we grabbed her until we ran the Zodiac up onto the beach on the town side of the causeway where we'd parked.

"Who are you. . . . I know you. . . . You were at my house. . . . What are you going to do. . . . My father will kill you. . . . What are you going to do to me. . . . My father will find me. . . . My father is going to kill you. . . ." With one of us on each arm we ran Bonnie up the beach and stuffed her into the backseat of Hawk's car. I got in with her. Hawk got in the front and drove it away with all deliberate speed.

On the ride to Cambridge, she kept it up.

"You better not hurt me. . . . If you touch me, my father will kill you. . . . Why are you doing this to me. . . . If you want money, my father will pay. . . . My father has tons of money. . . ."

The years of sun had not been kind to Bonnie's skin. It was deeply tanned and deeply weathered and rough with an infinity of small diamond-shaped wrinkles that you could only see if you were close. I was close. I didn't want her opening the door and jumping or lowering the window and screaming. I would have been pleased had she shut up, but it was, I supposed, one of the hazards of kidnapping.

We pulled into the driveway beside Susan's house and went past Junior's huge mass and up the back stairs to Susan's apartment. After he saw who we were, Junior showed no interest. I opened the back door with my key, and we went in. Pearl appeared from the bedroom, walking very low and growling and making very short barks until she saw that it was me. Then she bounded past Bonnie and jumped up as I'd often urged her not to do, put her paws on my shoulders, and gave sort of bitey kisses on the nose, some of which hurt. While I accepted my welcome from Pearl, Hawk sat Bonnie down in Susan's living room. It was almost five. Susan would be up from her last appointment in a little while.

"You'll be sorry," Bonnie said. "When my father finds you, you're going to be really, really sorry."

Pearl came bounding across the room and jumped up on the couch beside

Bonnie. Bonnie screamed. Pearl sniffed at her face and Bonnie huddled into a ball. Hawk looked amused. He made a little clucking noise to Pearl and she jumped off the couch and went over to him and the two of them sat in the big armchair and Hawk patted her. The front door opened and Vinnie Morris came in with a gun. He looked at me and Hawk and put the gun away. He paid no attention to Bonnie.

"I heard people moving around up here," Vinnie said.

"Where's Ty-Bop?" I said.

"Out front."

"And you're inside."

"Senior man," Vinnie said.

I nodded at Bonnie.

"Now," I said to Vinnie, "might be the time for extra alertness."

"Sure," Vinnie said and went back downstairs.

"Would you like a drink?" I said to Bonnie.

"Like whisky?"

I nodded.

"Yeah," she said. "Gimme some Chivas on the rocks."

I looked at Hawk. He grinned.

"Yassah, Boss," he said and shuffled off toward the kitchen where Susan kept her booze.

I got a straight chair and straddled it in front of Bonnie.

"Whaddya want with me, anyway?" Bonnie said. "You got any idea who I am. You got any idea what kinda trouble you got yourself into?"

"Yes," I said.

Hawk came back and handed Bonnie her drink. Holding the thick lowball glass in both hands, she took in a lot of it. She didn't seem to mind that it wasn't Chivas Regal. Hawk looked at her for a moment and went back to the kitchen.

"So why don't you say something?" Bonnie said.

"Do you prefer Bonnie or Bunny?" I said.

She stared at me for a moment. "You came to my house," she said. "It was you that came, and Ziggy and the guys chased you off."

"I left in a dignified manner," I said. "Bonnie or Bunny?"

"Bonnie."

Hawk came back in with a bucket of ice and a nearly full bottle of Dewar's Scotch. He put both on the coffee table near her.

"Please," she said, "let me go. My father will give you a lot of money and, honest to God, I won't tell anybody."

Susan came in. We all waited while Pearl loped wildly around the room and jumped up on Susan, even when Susan asked her not to. Finally, she got calm enough for anyone to speak.

"Here she is," Susan said, looking at Bonnie.

"Here she is," I said.

"Am I now an accessory to kidnapping."

"I would guess, yes," I said.

Bonnie drank some more Scotch. Susan's arrival heartened her a little. The sisterhood is strong.

"Who are you?" she said.

"I'm Susan."

"What kind of place is this?"

Susan smiled. "This is my home," she said.

"Why'd they bring me here?"

"I would guess several reasons," Susan said. "People would probably not think to look for you here. If they did, there are several men here with guns. And I think there was the thought that I might be helpful in talking with you."

Bonnie's glass was empty. She added more Scotch.

Susan looked at me. "That about right?"

"On the money," I said.

"Talking to me?"

"Yes," I said.

"That's all you want?"

"I need to know some things," I said.

She drank some Scotch. Susan had sounded reasonable. Now I sounded reasonable. Hawk had brought her whisky. The whisky made her feel better.

"Like what?" she said.

"What happened to Abner Fancy?"

I could see her throat tighten. She stared at me without speaking.

"Shaka," I said.

Her voice had a squeezed sound when she spoke.

"My fa . . . who?"

"Your father?" I said.

She shook her head.

"Your father killed him, or had it done," I said.

"No."

"Bonnie," Susan said. "Did your father kill Abner because of you?"

Bonnie shook her head and drank some Scotch.

"Because you had a liaison with a black man?"

Bonnie kept shaking her head, her head down, looking at the floor.

"Because you produced a mulatto child?"

Bonnie's head came up and her eyes widened.

"Whom you gave away?" Susan said. "To Emily Gordon?"

"You and your mother have been paying Barry Gordon cover-up money for years," I said.

"It was support," she said. "For Daryl."

I nodded. Susan sat in an armchair across from Bonnie. I sat in front of her. Hawk leaned against the wall behind Susan, his arms folded across his chest, his eyes steady on Bonnie, his face without expression. Bonnie was still an okay-looking woman. She had spent too much time in the sun, and it had coarsened her skin. And she had spent too much time being Sonny's daughter and Ziggy's wife, and it had coarsened her soul. But I could see why Leon had considered her a hot little bitch.

"Who killed her?" I said.

"Who . . . ?"

"Who killed Emily?"

"I don't know."

"You do," I said. "You were in the bank when it happened."

"I . . ." she drank some more Scotch. "I'm not going to talk about this."

"How about the white guy?"

"White guy?"

"In the bank?"

"Rob," she said. "He did it."

"Uh-huh? Where's Rob now?"

"I don't know."

"Shaka killed him," I said. "So that Rob wouldn't talk."

She drank some Scotch and nodded enthusiastically. "Yes," she said. "That's what happened."

"Shaka shot Rob," I said, "to keep Rob from confessing to the murder?"

She nodded again. She wasn't very bright, and the booze wasn't making her brighter. I shook my head.

"You killed her," I said.

"No," she said.

"Shaka was her lover. Rob was there on behalf of peace and love and an end to imperialist aggression. You used to be Shaka's honey and he knocked you up, then he dumped you for Emily. You shot her to get Shaka back."

Bonnie dropped her head again and began to cry.

"I can understand how that would feel," Susan said to her. "You loved him, bore him a child. Did you give the child away because he'd leave you if you didn't?"

Bonnie nodded without looking up, still crying.

"And then he took up with the woman who had the child."

Bonnie nodded again.

"Was he suddenly interested in the child?"

Nod. Susan smiled sadly.

"How awful," Susan said. "You gave away your child to be with Shaka, and the child became something that took him away from you."

Bonnie cried loudly now.

"For crissake," I said. "Lovers, children. You people passed each other around like Fritos."

"It was a different time," Susan said gently.

Bonnie raised her teary face and looked at Susan. "It was," she said. "It was different. And I loved him so much, and that little Jew bitch took him away from me and she used my own kid to do it."

"And you had no other choice," Susan said. "You had a gun and it was your chance."

"I loved him too much to let her have him."

"I understand," Susan said.

"She was gone, and the kid got sent back

to Barry and it was me and Shaka again."

"And Daddy killed him," I said.

She dropped her drink on the floor. The noise made Pearl jump and slink in behind Susan's chair. Susan put her hand back automatically and patted Pearl. Bonnie put her face in both hands and doubled over and began to rock back and forth, gasping for breath between the huge sobs that made her whole body shake.

"And gave you to Ziggy," I said.

She couldn't speak, but she nodded. We all sat. No one said anything.

Finally I said, "We'll send you home. When you are able to, call your father, and let me speak to him."

61

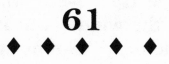

I was on the front porch of Susan's apartment when Sonny Karnofsky got out of the backseat of a black Mercedes sedan with tinted windows. Behind him was the Cadillac Escalade, also black and tinted. Menacing. Sonny stood alone next to his car and looked at me. On the porch behind me, Vinnie sat on the railing. Ty-Bop and Junior lounged in elaborate boredom next to him. Junior had a shotgun.

I walked down the steps to the sidewalk, and Sonny crossed the yard toward me. He looked old and tired in the bright sunlight.

"Where is she?" he said.

"Inside."

"Bring her out," he said.

"No. You come in."

Sonny was silent. I waited.

"Let me see her," Sonny said.

I nodded and waved my hand above my head. Susan's front door opened and Hawk stood in the doorway with Bonnie. Sonny looked at her silently for what seemed a long time. It was a hot day, I realized.

There was a persistent locust hum high up above us. The trees were still and full of substance in the windless heat.

"What's the deal?" Sonny said.

"You come in. We talk. You and Bonnie leave and we're square."

"What do we talk about."

"We got problems to resolve," I said.

Sonny was an ape. But he wasn't stupid. And he loved his daughter. He had no leverage and he knew it. We went into Susan's house and sat with Bonnie and Hawk in the downstairs study across from her office. Susan was downstairs. Bonnie didn't say anything, and after his first look Sonny didn't look at her again. He focused on me and waited.

"When Bonnie was eighteen," I said to him, "you sent her to college so she'd get an education and become a lady and be something besides the daughter of a thug."

Sonny's gaze was steady. The skin under his chin had sagged into a wattle, and his eyelids were so droopy that his eyes were slitted.

"But she fell in with the wrong crowd and turned into a hippie and dropped out. She got involved with drugs and sex and revolution. She had a fling with a black man and had a baby. She gave the baby

322

away to some other hippies named Emily and Barry Gordon. Later, she killed Emily during a bank robbery because she was jealous of her. Then she came back home in a panic."

Sonny's chin rested on his chest. He had his hands folded across his stomach. There were liver spots. His eyes were expressionless beneath the drooping lids. It was like being stared at by a turtle.

"Fortunately, the FBI had an informant involved in the bank robbery and didn't want it known. So they buried it. The people in the bank didn't see who did the shooting. The FBI informant was out in the getaway car. So only three people knew who shot Emily. Bonnie, a white guy named Rob, and a black con named Abner Fancy, who called himself Shaka."

"If it's true, I know all this," Sonny said. His voice sounded thick to me and kind of hoarse. "If it's not true, why are you telling me?"

"I want you to know what I know," I said. "Rob, the white peacenik, got shot as a precautionary measure by Shaka. And you had Shaka killed because he was the only one who knew that Bonnie killed Emily."

Sonny seemed to drop his chin farther.

But his gaze, now peering out from under his eyebrows, didn't falter. With his head down, I could see his pale scalp through the thin, white hair on top.

"And probably because he was a black ram, and he'd shtupped your white ewe."

"I don't know what the white ewe shit is all about," Sonny said. "But it don't matter. If what you're saying ain't true, then we got nothing to talk about. But say it is, then what?"

"That's what we have to work out. You got a granddaughter who doesn't know any of this and might not benefit from finding it out. She thinks she's the daughter of Emily and Barry Gordon. If she does find this stuff out, she shouldn't find it out in the context of her mother's trial for the murder of her stepmother, and her grandfather's trial for the murder of her father."

Bonnie sat completely still, staring at her father. It was a complicated look. Fear, dependence, maybe even affection, maybe some loathing, too.

"You can prove this?"

"That Bonnie killed Emily?" I said. "Hell, yes. But I don't see why I have to."

"Meaning?"

"Your daughter's been safely installed

with the lovely and charming Ziggy. If I could nail you with it I would, but that's not likely. Nobody's nailed you yet."

For a moment, Sonny almost looked pleased. But he recovered and gave me more of the flinty stare.

"So here's the deal. You see to it that no one bothers Susan, and I forget about Bonnie."

"I could kill you," Sonny said.

"And Martin Quirk gets this whole story," I said. "You know Quirk?"

"I know him."

"Anything happens to Susan, he gets the whole story."

"I agree to this and Bonnie walks," Sonny said.

"She does," I said. "Ziggy is punishment enough."

Sonny looked at his daughter. His look was probably as complicated as hers had been, but Sonny was used to not showing much, and it was hard to tell.

"Daddy?" Bonnie said in the kind of plaintive little girl voice that only a woman in her late fifties could actually produce.

Sonny nodded slowly to himself. He looked at Bonnie some more. Then he looked at me.

"Deal," he said and stood up.

He looked at his daughter again. "Come on," he said.

She looked at me. I made a be-my-guest gesture with my hand. She hesitated another moment, glanced at Hawk, and stood.

"Before you go," I said. "Just an idle question?"

Sonny stood and waited.

"Evan Malone," I said. "The FBI guy, retired in New Hampshire."

"Yeah?"

"You know where he is?"

"Yeah."

"Will I ever find him?"

"No."

I nodded. Hawk reached over and opened the study door. Sonny looked at his daughter and jerked his head.

"Have a nice life," I said.

And the Karnofskys walked out.

62

I was sitting on the top step of the front porch, watching people walk by on Linnaean Street, with Susan next to me and Hawk on the other side of her. I was drinking Blue Moon Belgian White Ale from the bottle. Susan and Hawk sipped Iron Horse champagne from proper crystal. Taste varies. A woman with long, straight hair and no makeup walked by in a formless ankle-length tan floral-print dress. Pearl the Wonder Dog II bounded about inside Susan's front fence, deciding on a basis none of us understood whom to bark at ferociously and whom to ignore. She decided to bark at the woman in the dress.

"Why has she decided to bark at her?" I said.

"I think it's the dress," Susan said

"I say it the whole look," Hawk said.

"That's the Cambridge look," Susan said.

"If that's the Cambridge look," I said, "what do they think of your look?"

"They think I'm a ho," Susan said.

Pearl stood with her forefeet on the top of the fence, glaring alertly down the street in the direction the woman had gone. The fur was stiff between her shoulder blades.

"Maybe the bodyguards were superfluous," I said.

"Everybody like Ty-Bop and Junior hanging on your front porch?" Hawk said.

"This is a very liberal community," Susan said.

"So how many people cross the street when they pass by your house?" Hawk said.

"Everybody."

Hawk smiled and sipped some champagne. He looked at me. "Now lemme see I got you straight," he said. "You and me shoot up almost anybody that move in eastern Massachusetts, so's we can find out who killed Emily Gordon."

"We did," I said.

Hawk nodded thoughtfully.

" 'Cause you promise Paul and Daryl you would."

"Yes."

"Even though Daryl tell you she don't want you to no more."

"She did say that."

"And then you finally find out who done it, and you make a deal with her and her old man and you let her go."

"You want to spend the rest of your life guarding Susan?" I said.

"Depends what else I got goin'," Hawk said. "But I get your point. You going to tell Daryl?"

"I don't know."

"If they wasn't a threat to Susan, would you have busted Sonny's daughter?"

I thought about that for a moment.

"He wouldn't have," Susan said.

"Tha's right," Hawk said.

Pearl bounded up onto the porch and squeezed in between me and Susan and sat down and lapped the top of my beer bottle.

"It's cool," I said, "having people answer their own questions for me. Saves thinking."

"Which be a good thing in your case," Hawk said. "Being as how you got so little to spare."

"Fine," I said. "And why did I stay on the case?"

"It like sex," Hawk said. "Don't want to pull out 'fore you finished."

"Rich imagery," I said.

"He's right, though," Susan said. "You can't quit early."

"You should know," I said.

"I do," she said. "You have no way to know until you get to the end, what the end is going to be."

"You sound like Yogi Berra."

"When you get to the end, then you decide. But you have to get to the end. You have to know how it will turn out."

"Because?" I said.

"Because it's how you are," Susan said.

"Which is?"

"Weird," Hawk said.

I looked at Susan. "More or less," she said.

I drank some beer. Hawk poured some more champagne for himself and Susan. Pearl lapped some champagne out of Susan's glass and shook her head and sneezed.

"Now that we've settled that," I said, "maybe we could return to the subject of pulling out."

Susan looked at me and smiled her wonderfulness-with-a-touch-of-evil smile.

"Or perhaps, later on, the reverse," she said.

About the Author

◆ ◆ ◆ ◆ ◆

Robert B. Parker is the bestselling author of more than forty books. He lives in Boston.

We hope you have enjoyed this Large Print book. Other Thorndike, Wheeler or Chivers Press Large Print books are available at your library or directly from the publishers.

For more information about current and up-coming titles, please call or write, without obligation, to:

Publisher
Thorndike Press
295 Kennedy Memorial Drive
Waterville, ME   04901
Tel. (800) 223-1244

Or visit our Web site at:
www.gale.com/thorndike
www.gale.com/wheeler

OR

Chivers Large Print
published by BBC Audiobooks Ltd
St James House, The Square
Lower Bristol Road
Bath BA2 3SB
England
Tel. +44(0) 800 136919
email: bbcaudiobooks@bbc.co.uk
www.bbcaudiobooks.co.uk

All our Large Print titles are designed for easy reading, and all our books are made to last.